THIS BOOK ISN'T FAT, IT'S FABULOUS

THIS BOOK ISN'T FAT, IT'S FABULOUS

THIS BOOK
ISN'T FAT,
IT'S

Fabulous

NINA
BECK

Point

Library of Congress Cataloging-in-Publication Data
Beck, Nina.
This book isn't fat, it's fabulous / by Nina Beck. — 1st ed.
p. cm.
Summary: Sixteen-year-old Riley Swain, pushed into spending Spring Break at an upstate New York "fat farm" by her father's fiancée, is happy with her weight but finds she has a lot to learn about friendship and love.
ISBN-13: 978-0-545-01703-9 (alk. paper)
ISBN-10: 0-545-01703-3 (alk. paper)
[1. Interpersonal relations — Fiction. 2. Boarding schools — Fiction. 3. Schools — Fiction. 4. Self-esteem — Fiction. 5. Overweight persons — Fiction. 6. New York (N.Y.) — Fiction. 7. New York (State) — Fiction.] I. Title: This book is not fat it is fabulous. II. Title.

PZ7.B380783Thi 2008
[Fic] — dc22

2007048889

Book design by Christopher Stengel

12 11 10 9 8 7 6 5 4 3 2 1   8 9 10 11 12 13/0
Printed in the U.S.A.

First edition, September 2008

For Dieter Galt — D, this is just one
of the many perks of being my
best friend. Just an FYI.

FABULOUS

THIS BOOK ISN'T FAT, IT'S FABULOUS

Aaron Tremaine, Esq.
Swain Corporate Headquarters
Legal Department
1020 Park Avenue | 13th Floor
New York, NY 10001

Dear Mr. Tremaine,

I'm writing to inform you that my father's fiancée, Ms. Elizabeth Butler (of the Boston Butlers), is plotting to take over Swain Corp. I believe that Ms. Butler is planning on getting me "out of the way" so she can take advantage of my father's advanced years and sexual dependency.

Although I have no hard evidence – I've enclosed a copy of an application to New Horizons, where I believe the aforementioned Elizabeth Butler has connections and has (abusing the aforementioned personality flaws) convinced my father to send me for the entire spring break. I've already discussed this issue with my father, and I believe that he is beyond help – perhaps having been brainwashed. Can you brainwash someone through their PDA? If so, my father is definitely at risk – so I suggest that you discreetly investigate Ms. Elizabeth Butler. If you need a witness in order to prosecute, I'll be happy to volunteer.

Also, when you have a moment, could you please send me information on petitioning for emancipation?

Thank you for your time.

Sincerely,

Riley Swain
xoxo

Riley Swain

Encl: New Participant Information Sheet; New Horizons, programs for young ladies Brochure; Picture of Elizabeth Butler asleep, drooling.

NEW HORIZONS
PROGRAM FOR YOUNG LADIES

NEW Participant Information Sheet

We're *so* excited to have you joining us at the New Horizons: Program for Young Ladies! Please take a moment to fill out this important information sheet so we can get a chance to know you prior to your arrival. Based on your answers, we will be making room arrangements and schedules, so please be honest and open with your responses. If you have any questions or concerns, feel free to contact Jen Brent at New Horizons. Ext 203. See you soon!

NAME   Riley Swain

AGE/BIRTHDAY   16/ October 18

WEIGHT   186–188 (depending on if I'm on the scale naked or not)

HEIGHT   Five feet, six and three-quarter inches tall (but I look taller naked)

BODY TYPE   Statuesque & pear-shaped

HOMETOWN   Manhattan (the best city in the world)

REASON FOR ATTENDING NEW HORIZONS

    I was tricked. In fact, you should keep this sheet as evidence because I have already filed a complaint through my lawyer and he'll probably be calling any day now.

GOALS FOR YOUR FIRST YEAR 1. Convince Johnny Depp to marry me. 2. Seduce Johnny Depp or Orlando Bloom — or basically anyone who had a role in *Pirates of the Caribbean* — at this point I'll even consider a key grip. 3. Talk to a shrink about my compulsive need to shock strangers by discussing my future sexual conquests on stupid "new participant information sheets." 4. Gain twelve pounds — and find a man who loves a woman with thighs that rub together.

FAVORITE AFTER-SCHOOL ACTIVITIES 1. Theater (in NY) 2. Music (in NY) 3. Hanging out with friends (who live in NY — and by "New York" I don't mean this out-in-the-middle-of-nowhere Bangor, NY; I mean, THE New York — Manhattan).

FAVORITE FOOD Is this a trick question?

DO YOU HAVE ANY RELIGIOUS OR PERSONAL PREFERENCES IN REGARDS TO MEALS? My personal religious preference is that I must eat chocolate chip cookie dough ice cream when I have my period. Everything else is negotiable — except I don't (DO NOT) eat lima beans. Ever.

DO YOU PREFER HAVING A MALE OR FEMALE DOCTOR? Depends, how old is he? HA-HA! Just kidding. Male. Any age is fine. XOXO

WHAT IS YOUR FAVORITE SUBJECT IN SCHOOL? Drama, math (but not geometry. That's not math anyway, that's art), and sometimes English.

NEW HORIZONS

PROGRAM FOR YOUNG LADIES

New Horizons is a yearlong boarding school program for young ladies. While we specialize in education and lifestyle maintenance for young ladies with body image issues or eating disorders, our excellent facilities and low staff-to-student ratio make us a prime school for many regional students. Each spring break we host a special two-week program for our full-time students who decide to remain on campus when classes break and for a few select nonprogram youths. This often gives an excellent introduction to the New Horizons program, by offering the same schedule and complementary programs that students receive during the year, in our wonderful buildings and campus.

A Sample Itinerary Includes*

7–8 A.M.: Breakfast

Enjoy breakfast in our award-winning cafeteria — designed by local architect Sam Scheck.

8:30–9: Meetings with Behavioral Coach

During the school year, students will meet daily with their group, but we like to keep it a little more personal during the spring break sessions.

9–11: Free Activity Period

Students can choose among any number of fun and interesting activities, including art classes, theater, clubs, or sports!

Noon: Lunch

2–3 P.M.: Seminar

Educational Period in the auditorium

3:30–5: Physical Education in our gym

We have separate weight rooms and a lap pool for our students.

5:30–7: Dinner

7–10: Quiet Time

11: Lights-out

The girls stay in our fabulous Victoria Dormitory, which has been outfitted recently with WiFi for student convenience. Of course, if they are interested in pursuing an academic project during their time here, our college-level research library has everything they will ever need.

Please join us for orientation at noon. We've included a map and a train schedule. We'll be running a shuttle from the eleven o'clock train arrival.

We look forward to welcoming you onto our campus!

*All activities are subject to change.

LIMERENCE

I have an important theory about love. My theory is that if you fall in love with your best friend, or if your best friend is everything you're looking for in a guy (and the list is a long and complicated one, so there are only — like — three guys on the planet who would be eligible for the position of "Mr. Perfect" anyway) . . . and if you fall in love with him and he doesn't fall in love with you . . . he should at least have the decency to be gay.

Seriously.

But Michael D. Hammond III ("D" for short) is not gay. He's smart, good-looking, and can be charming when he wants to be.

By that I mean that I've seen him be charming with other girls. And when I whine that he's not nearly so charming to me, he holds my hand and smiles like I've said something darling, like he's a proud parent and his little girl just said a bad word without knowing it was a bad word and isn't she precocious? And then he'll say something devastating like, "Darling, you're my soul mate; I'd never lie *to you* that way."

And then he'll kiss me on the forehead and I die. But on the surface? I just roll my eyes and say something bitchy to keep him from seeing how much it kills me when he says stuff like that.

Which makes me sound like a pathetic loser.

But the truth is that D knows how I feel about him, so the reality of the situation is that he's a jerk, I'm a masochist, and we're best friends.

And in a perfectly girl-psychotic manner, I feel the need to date and obsess over other guys in front of him. To taunt him with the idea of losing me to some other guy — not just my friendship but the wonderful future I've created in my imagination in which he realizes my brilliance, my charm, my wit, the something that makes me special.

I waste all my charm and flirting and brilliance on other guys, always for his benefit. I've perfected the art of getting the guy I don't want, which most people find amazing, considering the fact that I'm a size 10 (okay, 12, whatever). And when you're "fat" you're not supposed to get guys. But when you're desperately in love, anything is possible and although I couldn't give a fig for these guys . . . they are there, litter on the ground, dust in my wake, casualties of unreciprocated love. Theirs, mine, ours.

I know that as long as D's around I will never be able to look at another guy without thinking that he isn't the one I want. And I wonder if I'll ever fall out of love with D.

If only D had the good sense to like men. All of this could've been avoided.

THINGS I HATE
ABOUT MY BODY

It's a relatively short list, considering what the media would have me believe is wrong with my body. I like my boobs — although I hate the fact that I call them boobs, even in my own head.

Breasts seems too much like something your health teacher would call them. *Tits,* fifth-grade boy. What's left? *Bazongas?* Sure, why not? I like my bazongas. Although I'm pretty sure my left one is a half cup larger than my right one.

In the eighth grade I looked this up on the Internet and it's a common thing — one being bigger than the other — but I'm still obsessed with it. I think it has something to do with me being a righty, so I spent a year (ninth grade) trying to write with my left hand — or rather, I did this until my teachers all complained and my grades started dropping because nobody could read my homework or test answers.

So I hate my left bazonga but like my bazongas in general.

I like my legs. I think my front teeth could be a bit larger — but they are straight without the benefit of braces. So those are just mild annoyances. My second toe is smaller than my big toe, a fact for which I praise God every day. But — all of my fingers are the same size. They aren't particularly meaty fingers or anything, but they are literally ALL the same size (except the pinky is a little smaller). I can wear my rings on ANY finger. This bothers me. I point it out whenever I wear rings.

I also have incredible hearing. I hate that.

MARLEY DIGGONS IS A GRADE-A BITCH

Rumors have been flying over why I'm not going on the senior trip to Mexico, especially since I'm the one who planned the whole thing. There were fourteen of us going for the second week of spring break. Fourteen out of the thirty-six juniors in our class and fourteen out of the fourteen who were actually invited to attend.

My favorite rumor so far is that I'm going to visit a seer in Scotland to speak with my dead mother. Others range from rehab (which is popular these days) to going on a love tryst with one of our teachers from Curtis Prep. As if. But I guess it's better that they think I'm shacking up with Mr. O'Brien (the closest thing to a hot teacher there is at CP) than know the truth.

I'm a little miffed that no one is really upset that I'm not going. Marley Diggons is absolutely ecstatic.

Marley Diggons, aside from the role as Grade-A Bitch, is also a pinch-faced twit and my best friend. Or should I say best enemy? D is always asking why I don't tell her to take a flying leap, but things like that don't happen on the Upper East Side.

You keep your friends close, your boyfriend closer, and your best enemy so close, people think you're conjoined twins. That way you know when she's talking shit about you and you can combat it quickly and effectively as you whisper your own little subtle death threats in her ear.

Plus, we've known each other forever. My dad is always asking me:

How's Marty Diggons's girl?

Me: Oh, Mary is fine, Dad!

How's that girl of Marty Diggons? You two still friends?

Me: Oh, Martha and I are best friends, Daddy!

I saw Marty Diggons today, he asked after you. How's his daughter doing?

Me: Oh, Melanie is lovely as always. Turning into quite the young lady.

And my dad would nod from behind his newspaper, never looking up. If he ever noticed that Marley-Mary-Martha-Melanie's name changed on a regular basis, he never mentioned it. I wonder if Marley does the same thing with her dad?

MD: How's Richard Swain's daughter doing?

Marley: Oh, Riley? She's turned into the biggest tramp in the history of Curtis Prep. She took on half the student body and a few of the younger faculty members last week at the pep rally. It was stunning.

MD: That's nice, dear (as he gives the paper a good flick to straighten the pages while he reads the finance section).

We've remained best enemies for the sakes of our dads. Sometimes parents can be such trials.

But procedure and protocol on best enemies are still very loose. It means that I still invite her to my Christmas party when all of our parents take off for drinks at the Waldorf. Every year she receives an eggshell-colored card with delicate script (all calligraphy done by hand, of course) announcing the X-annual Christmas Party hosted by Miss Riley Swain at her residence. This is out of respect for my father. If it was up to me, I would've stopped inviting her after the eighth grade when she got absolutely smashed on cheap vodka and made out with Andrew Benjamin Thompson. Seriously.

I'm sure you've seen pictures of Benji and Angela (his girl-friend, sort of) in the Hamptons society pages. They've been dating forever, their parents are best friends, and everyone expects them to get engaged when they go off to Yale together next year. Little do they know that Benji is completely and utterly gay. Even Angie knows. But what's she going to do? There aren't that many acceptable men at Curtis Prep (four) and everyone knows it is better to have a boyfriend who goes to the gym as much to check out the eye candy as to do thigh workouts than it is to be dateless.

Anyway, Marley and Benji made out. Angela found out and didn't speak with Marley for exactly two weeks. It was hilarious; I think Marley was more freaked out than Angela was upset. But now it's just an embarrassing episode that nobody brings up, but that's just because they don't know that I have video from my camera-phone of Benji telling Marley to speak in a lower voice while she touched his you-know-what.

I'm still trying to figure out how to deliver that particular gift.

Perhaps for graduation? Text it over to their parents?

I'm almost loathe to call off the tenuous truce that Marley and I have.

We made it when we got a little tipsy at Tricia Owens's birthday party and I admitted to being in love with D and she admitted that she got breast augmentation done because she had an inverted nipple. We've been doing so well that I'm ashamed to admit that I was actually shocked when I overheard her talking about my trip to upstate New York.

I arrive at this party fashionably late (as usual). I barely can make it through the marble entryway of the town-house apartment. There are already so many people crammed into the apartment, mostly people I know from school, but every once in a while I see eyes that I don't recognize as they linger above the veil of a tipped-back martini glass.

I can barely hear the clink of my kitten heels against the marble foyer as I try to make my way back to the booze in the living room bar (usually where I find my friends congregating) when I spot them huddled into a corner settee — half hidden by a hideously fake palm tree. I wonder who they are hiding from and gossiping about.

What's that old saying? Curiosity killed the cat? Well, if curiosity killed the cat, gossip revived her and then ran over her with a Mack truck.

Cynthia Juel-Roberts: *I heard she's going to rehab.* (Side note: CJR drinks like a fish . . . but at least she holds her liquor better than her mother.)

Amanda SomethingOrOtherBecauseShe'sNotImportant EnoughToRemember: *I heard her father is sending her to a military academy for what happened last month with Edward.* (I don't want to talk about it. Let's just say the rumors about Edward Junior are completely true.)

Marley: *Amanda, don't be retarded. That was a month ago.*

For a second I don't realize they are talking about me. Even I'm not so egocentric that I believe everyone talks about me every minute of the day (just most people, most min-utes . . . ha-ha). I figure it out when Amanda Something says the thing about Edward. But Marley? Sticking up for me? This obviously shocks me. Truce doesn't necessarily mean that we go around protecting each other from the opinions and backstabbing of other girls. We just don't actively participate. While this is a minor shock, the major shock comes when she continues.

Marley: *. . . I hear her dad is sending her to fat camp.*

I hear two sharp intakes of breath and then a high-pitched giggle (CJR, bitch).

Marley: . . . *And not a moment too soon.*

I walk away. They haven't seen me.

I mean, it's one thing to talk about how a girl in your circle of friends is an absolute slut. Or if she drinks like a fish and most nights will be found vomiting in the nearest bathroom or offering the first guy she sees a hand job to drive her home (CJR), or if she role-plays as a boy with a gay guy her friend is dating (MD). But there are some things that should be sacred among women.

Apparently not.

So I do the only thing I can think of doing. I push myself through the throng of people whose faces begin to look all Monet and smeared (I am NOT going to cry) and I do the one thing I know how to do well. I go looking for revenge. I go looking for Marley's crush.

THIS PARTY SUCKS, AND THE LOVE OF MY LIFE

Having made my escape and my plan for revenge, I blink away my tears fast enough to notice a picture of Amanda Something with two Older Somethings and the ugliest dog I've ever seen hanging in a portrait above the fireplace in the living room. I grab a glass of half-drunk red wine off the banister that separates part of the living room where there is a baby grand piano. Which obviously has never been played. Pretension, above all things, makes me sick. You can't fake the bitchiness that comes with breeding. I should know.

We're all at Amanda Something's house. Which is why I guess *she's* here. Her parents are probably away at a weekend spa retreat and Amanda is taking advantage of their absence in an attempt to raise her social status. And it is working. For the weekend. She's still not invited on my Mexico trip and by Monday she'll have faded better than the wine stain I'm about to leave on her mom's white rug.

I step behind the baby grand and spill a little bit of wine out and it seeps into the carpet, leaving a deep red stain. Enough? Perhaps. I tip the glass a little more and begin drawing it in the shape of two overly large breasts.

I leave the glass there, stepping back to see my artistic handiwork, and smile. Then I bend down and wipe my finger-prints off the glass — which I admit might be overdoing it a little, but you never know . . . better safe than sorry.

I feel this is fitting retribution for what she has said.

Not that I'm still thinking about that. Instead I'm focused on finding Timothy. He's around here somewhere, probably with the rest of the crew team, trying to look cool while they wait for their girlfriends to get drunk enough to screw them.

I make my way through a group of people I don't even know and into the kitchen to pour myself a drink (using a plastic cup, how lame). There isn't even a bar here. I'm shaking my head sadly when I spot D sitting on a lounge a few feet away from me. He's wearing a red satin kimono tied over a tight black T-shirt and Diesel jeans.

I know what you're thinking . . . a kimono? WTF? But seriously. If anyone can pull it off, it's D.

"Have a cobble-squat, sweetheart," he says in the cutest Brit accent ever. He always says that he attributes at least ninety-five percent of the play he gets to the fact that he pronounces words like *basil* "bah-zil." Apparently all women (on this side of the Atlantic) get hot hearing *bah-zil*. I know I do.

"Thanks." I give him a kiss on the cheek and he holds out his drink, which I take and drink down — almost all of it — before he has a chance to grab it back. "I just overheard Marley and everyone talking about why I'm not going on spring break with you guys."

D stops with his glass to his lips, tilted up but not drinking. He quirks an eyebrow. Have I mentioned he's hot? Have I mentioned that I haven't told him why I'm not going and that even though he's dying of curiosity, I would rather swallow my own tongue than tell him the truth?

"I'm either going to military school, rehab, or screwing Mr. O'Brien."

He relaxes his shoulders and smiles at me before finishing the last sip of liquid.

"Marley's a bitch," I add.

"Guess the truce is off, then?" he asks.

"Yup."

"She's a pinch-faced twit." (Note that this sounds way better coming out of his mouth with the Brit accent than it did in my NY brain. But I was used to that.)

"That she is. And now she'll be a Timless pinch-faced twit."

D sighs and puts down the glass. I see Marley across the room, drinking, still sitting by the palm with her (our) friends, and Timothy standing on the other side of the room, having just walked in with the rest of the crew team from somewhere in the back of the apartment, probably doing drugs in Amanda

14

Something's bathroom. One or more people will have undoubtedly puked in there before the end of this party, probably missing the toilet, and Amanda will be grossed out when she realizes, but she'll probably call the housekeeper and think it was well worth it. Sure that she'll be more popular by Monday (nope) and her parents will never be the wiser (double nope).

Marley must've caught me staring because she smiles slightly and does a little wave-over. I smile back, shake my head, and hold up a finger. One minute, darling.

"Riley," D says. "You don't have to get involved with this. Just ignore her."

"I will, but just after one thing." I get up and straighten my skirt and make my way over to the crew team.

WHY THE CREW TEAM JOCKS ARE DUMBER THAN ALL THE OTHER JOCKS AT CP COMBINED

Last year all the crew guys convinced Andy Brince to steal a copy of the English final, which was really screwed up since Andy's the only guy on the team who needs his scholarship. But it's an athletic scholarship — which means he's not any smarter than the rest of them. He gets a copy of an English exam and they all memorize the answers on the stolen paper. The next week they walk into English, sit down, and take the test, apparently without really looking at it. Just a bunch of dumb jocks filling in circles with their number twos.

Each of them answers the test with the exact same answers (you'd think they'd at least try to make it look like they weren't cheating) ... but I guess it would've been fine if they had all gotten 100's. A miracle, yes, but they would've gotten away with it — if they had been taking the English

FINAL and not the English midterm that Andy Brince stole from the drawer.

Andy Brince is an idiot.

They all had to make up the test, but nobody got expelled, not even Andy Brince. It's hard to expel an entire team without their parents (or the alumni) complaining. Go, Cougars!

HOW TO SEDUCE
A DUMB JOCK

Hi, boys," I say as I walk up to the group.

The other guys say hey, but I smile directly at Timothy and he looks a little flustered.

RULE 1: MAKE EYE CONTACT EARLY AND OFTEN.

"Do you boys mind if I steal Tim here for a minute? I have something I want to talk to him about." The guys shrug and one guy does that weird eyebrow waggle at him, like he's implying something — but when I look at him, he drops the look and waits for me to yell at him. Instead I just smile. Timothy falls in behind me and I look over and see Marley staring at him and me, walking out of the room together. If she was smart, she'd get over here right now and cut us off.

But Marley's an idiot.

I pull Timothy into the hallway, toward the bathroom and probably the bedrooms. He seems really uncomfortable so I look over my shoulder and smile at him. He looks confused. Probably because I've never said more than a word to him.

We're standing farther down in the hall, a spot where we're out of the direct line of vision of the rest of the party, but anyone could still come down the hall and see us together (and run and tell Marley). The walls are a strange green color and are covered with family photos that show Amanda Something and the Something Dog at various stages of childhood. Amanda Something used to be a really cute kid. Too bad she's a bitch now.

"So, eh . . . (add, like, five minutes of stuttering in here) . . . I hear, like, you're um, not, like, going on the, um, like, trip." Tim smiles at the end of his sentence like he just peed for the first time in the big boy's toilet and for a second I wonder if I should set him up with Marley and that would be punishment enough.

RULE 2: MAKE HIM FEEL SMART AND IMPORTANT. EVEN IF HE'S NOT. ESPECIALLY IF HE'S NOT.

"Yeah, it's a bummer," I say, standing close to him. "But when your parents want to drag you to Scotland, what are you going to do?"

He nods. "Yeah, that sucks."

"Anyway, I'm really disappointed because I wanted us to get to know each other better."

19

"What? Really? What?"

He looks charmingly confused and so I smile. I don't want to crush him. I just want to kiss him. Marley and I have this unspoken rule that if one of us kisses a guy, the other will consider him tainted by all the evil in the world and not touch him with a ten-foot pole. She kissed Marc Jennings in the sixth grade and when I had to kiss him during Spin the Bottle a few weeks later, I thought I was going to vomit.

I pull Tim into a small library off the hallway, closing the door behind us. I couldn't do this in front of all those small, staring Amanda Somethings. Her little Something Dog was giving me the willies.

"You know I think you're really cute, right?"

Rule 3: When all else fails, be obvious.

He nods enthusiastically for a second, then stops.
"Um . . ." he says.

Rule 4: Really, really obvious.

"Look, I'm kinda nervous, you know. I don't know if you find me attractive at all. . . ." I pause.

"Actually, I think you're really cute." He shoots me a shy smile. I hate being called cute.

"Really?" I gush.

"Yeah, I mean, I always thought so," he says, warming to his chosen subject. "I like big girls." He coughs once and looks up at me from behind his too-long lashes. Wait, correction. He was looking down my top.

I say: "Um . . ."

Because that's all I could think of . . . *I like big girls?* I'm not sure if that was a compliment or if I should be offended. This isn't in the rule book.

Timothy is the product of too much upper-class inbreeding. When too many dumb rich kids drink too much with other dumb rich kids, go yachting, and kiss one another on the cheeks (or better yet, on the air by their cheeks), this is the sort of child they produce. If nothing else, I'm against a class system for this very reason.

But I am still standing there in shocked silence.

He stands up and put his hands on my shoulders. I am in the perfect position to knee him in the groin. Instead I let him kiss me.

RULE 5: PRETEND TO BE INTO IT.

I might have flubbed this one. Here is the transcript of my brain while I let Marley's crush kiss me:

He was just drinking Heineken. Who drinks Heineken? I can't breathe when he covers my mouth that way. I wonder if I tilt my head if I could breathe better. This is annoying. Someone should tell him to control his saliva glands when he kisses. Ew, I think I just swallowed his spit. Ew. I wonder what Marley will say when —

And then he presses against me and his hands begin kneading my bazongas, hard, and I freak out.

"Um, yeah," I say, backing away from him, pulling his hands out from under my shirt. Slippery little sucker. He is smiling. I am wiping my mouth with my fingertips (I want to wipe it on my shirt, spit a little, get some mouthwash . . .).

"Well, this is . . . was . . . um, great. I'll talk to you later," I say, trying to think quickly.

He just sits there and smiles in a skeevy way and my stomach flips over.

"Um. Yeah," I say, and I turn around and run from the room.

When I get back out to the party, Marley is gone.

I walk outside. I need some cool air. I feel gross. Really gross. I wonder what Marley thinks. I wonder what Timothy is thinking. It almost doesn't matter because all I can picture is that smile that makes me want to scratch his face off. I'm going to go home and boil my bra. No, I'll throw it in the fireplace. Which doesn't make any sense. I *wanted* him to kiss me. I wanted to kiss him. Or, at the very least, I wanted Marley to think that we kissed. Why do I feel so gross?

I get outside Amanda Whatever's brownstone and D's standing there with some guy in a leather bomber jacket — dude, it's spring — smoking a cigarette. He sees my face and nods at the other guy, cutting him off midsentence. The other guy, some kid I don't know, looks perplexed and then looks over at me and just nods and goes back inside. Sometimes I forget that guys have their own non-word-based communication like girls do. Girls are just better at it.

When the guy is gone, D just shakes his head at me.

"I'm not sure if I love you for being completely devoid of all sense of morality or if I should be appalled by your behavior."

I almost burst into tears, the second time in one night. I must be PMSing. Instead I flash him a grin, twirl around, and curtsy deeply so I can blink back my tears without him seeing.

"I'm sure it wouldn't matter either way," I snap, before walking to the curb to look up and down the street for a cab. It's warm; a lot of people are out tonight.

We're somewhere in the Village and I'm surprised we even came this far downtown for a party, but I must admit that Amanda Something has a pretty nice place, for the neighborhood. There is a pretty little café on the corner that has a few people standing outside of it, smoking, kissing, laughing. Cars are parked on the side of the street, and on the other side of the street a couple is strolling really slowly toward some destination that they obviously don't want to reach.

"Everything OK?" D asks.

I feel him staring at the back of my head and for a minute I want to tell him everything. How I hate Marley. How I really

23

hate Timothy. And how he's the only one who cares about me and how I love him and that . . .

"Yeah, of course," I say. "Want to share a cab?"

I send messages with my eyes, asking him to come with me. Or, at the very least, to ask me what is wrong. One more time and I'll confess everything.

"I don't think so," he says. "Marley is still inside."

"So?"

"Well," he says as I turn around to face him. "She might be needing some . . ." He smiles, shrugs. I think I just stopped breathing. Again.

"And I'm the one devoid of all sense of morality?"

He smiles at me behind a brush of long black bangs that falls over his eyes. Women are always falling for that smile. The problem with D is that he looks at you like you're different. Like you're worth smiling with, like you're the first and last person he'll ever want to smile at.

It's a lie. He smiles at me like that now, and he's my best friend — nothing more — and he's about to go in and make out with Marley Diggons, and give her the same smile, when he should know that it's going to kill me to think of them together.

But it's not like I can say that. I have absolutely no place to say who he can and cannot make out with. I'm his best friend. I'm the only girl he spends any time with, I'm different — he says. But he's not interested in me *that* way. If I start making demands, well, I might just lose my best friend too.

"Go get her, tiger," I say, giving him a nudge back toward the front door. "Just remember what happened with Benji." I give him a pointed look at his crotch and he pretends to cringe and cover his privates, limping back toward the door.

"Will I talk to you before I go?"

"Most definitely. When are you leaving?"

"Tomorrow morning, ten A.M."

"Most definitely not. Couldn't they pack you off at a decent hour?"

He walks over to me and gives me a kiss and a hug. I feel it to my bones but I push away first. He quirks his head at me and then laughs. He's used to me pushing him away. He thinks I'm prickly, that I don't like people touching me. But the truth is I want him. He smells good. I feel like if I don't push away first, I won't be able to push away at all. I'd hold on too long, and especially tonight, it just feels different. I don't want to ruin it. I push away.

I'm still wondering what it would be like to kiss D.

"Go. I'm sure Marley's crying in her martini by now."

"What kind of gentleman would I be if I didn't save a fair maiden from a watered-down martini?"

I hate Marley Diggons.

"Good night, darling. Have fun in upstate New York."

I shush him and get into the cab. I hate Marley Diggons with every essence of my being. I hope her birth control mixes badly with her antidepressants. I hope her hairdresser has a seizure while she's doing her six-week trim and cuts a chunk off the back of her head. I hope her roots grow out abnormally fast. I hope she gets nail fungus. . . .

I turn and watch Michael standing half in and half out of the door, waving down the street at me. I wave back.

I hope . . . that she has already left or is hooking up with someone else.

I.M. CONVERSATION, FOUR A.M. I SHOULD BE SLEEPING. I'M WAITING UP FOR D.

RILEDUP: . . . and then I just left.

THEBIGUN17: Just like that? You didn't say anything to him?

RILEDUP: He should've known.

THEBIGUN17: Yeah, cause guys are natural mind readers. We always know when chicks are freaking about something, that's why we're such good communicators. You should give this guy a break and tell him how you feel.

RILEDUP: You're like a mind reader.

THEBIGUN17: No, I'm not.

RILEDUP: Yeah, you always know the right thing to say to me. And we've never even met. It's like, I can really be honest with you in a way I can't be with anyone else.

THEBIGUN17: That's just because we've never met.

RILEDUP: I don't know, I think we'd be just as good friends in

27

person. I mean, we've been talking for almost four months now and I feel like you know more about me than some of my best friends.

THEBIGUN17: Well, maybe one day we'll test that theory out.

RILEDUP: Oh! D's calling. I GG. THX for listening to me whine!

THEBIGUN17: No prob. Later.

THE EPISODE WHERE I MAKE OUT WITH D (NOT TO RUIN THE ENDING OR ANYTHING)

I text D around four and he calls me back.

"So did you rescue the fair maiden from a watered-down martini?"

"Didn't find her," he says and for a second I feel somewhat elated.

"Wow, so you went home alone for once?"

He just laughs. "I didn't say *that*, I just said I didn't go home with Marley."

"You're such a slut."

"Proudly so," he slurs into the phone. I smile.

"Are you drunk?"

"Proudly so."

I laugh into the phone. "Coming over?" I ask. D is already waiting downstairs by the time I get there. Of course, it had taken me twenty minutes just to make my way downstairs. I had to brush my teeth, do my hair, pull on my ass-jeans (the ones that make my ass look awesome), brush on just enough makeup to make it look like I didn't have any makeup but was still, you know, in color. Add a few spritzes of body spray. Flip my hair upside down, give it a good shake and then flip it right side up again, and walk down the front steps, where he sits smoking a cigarette.

"Hey," he says, giving me a glance. He holds out his cigarette to me, which I shake off.

"Why are you up?" I ask.

"Why are you up?" he asks back.

"Just thinking about stuff," I say.

He nods and flicks some ashes onto the ground. He has his elbows on his knees and is looking out at the street and the occasional car that drives past. "You know you're my best friend, right?"

I sigh. I don't want to get into the whole affirmation-of-friendship thing. I want to shake him and scream, *I can love you better than any other person on the face of the planet, even when you're being an egocentric jerk!*

"Why are you sighing?" he asks, turning to look at me. He looks seriously upset.

"You're really drunk," I say. "I don't want to do the relationship-analysis thing tonight."

"Like we do it all the time."

"We do," I say. "I mean, maybe not together, but I do a lot of relationship analysis."

He looks at me, curious for a moment, and then takes another drag off of his cigarette.

"Is that so?" he finally asks.

"Yes." I take the cigarette from him, which is, like, all ash by now and flick it onto the sidewalk. He takes out another and lights it.

"What is it that you analyze?" he asks.

"Why you don't like me."

"Huh?"

Holy shit, did I just say that aloud?

"Of course I like you, you're my best friend," he says, and pushes me slightly with the side of his body. I don't rock over and then rock back into him, like I usually do. This is like Eskimo kisses for friends. This is the "are we cool?" motion. I sit straight and don't sway.

"You know I'm mostly, sort of in love with you," I say softly.

He doesn't say anything for a minute, he sighs, he coughs, he looks around, hoping for a bomb to fall from the sky in order to keep him from having to answer this question.

"Yeah," he says, finally.

"And you don't love me."

"You're wrong," he says. "I love you."

31

I laugh, because even though I know what he's saying — it's a rejection — it doesn't matter tonight. Which is weird, and tomorrow I'm sure he'll still remember all of this despite my hope that it'll all disappear in a drunken, smoky haze.

"Riley, look at me," he says, and I turn to face him. "I do love you. I mean, who was the only person I could talk to about the stuff with my parents? Who do I spend all my time with? Who do I go see at four A.M. when I can't sleep? I love you — I just don't love you that way."

"I get it." But I don't. I mean, he's never even kissed me . . . how can he be sure that he doesn't want me if he hasn't even tried? We obviously get along really well. We obviously love each other as friends — doesn't it just make sense that if all that is there, that we should try this other thing too?

"Maybe . . ."

"Forget it, D, this is silly," I say, and I can feel myself starting to get all emotional again. I feel like it's all just happening at once, and it's late and I feel like the darkness is a shield and I can say anything and I'm not embarrassed. I think back to how much alcohol I consumed earlier. Not enough. "Do you ever think about kissing me?"

"Yes," he says. His eyes stay out on the road. My eyes are bugging out. YES? He says yes and doesn't feel the need to follow up? *Pardonnez-moi?* Maybe if I wait him out, he'll say something.

He finishes his cigarette and tosses it into the street.

"Well, good night. Have a great trip," he says, standing up and wiping his hands on the sides of his jeans.

"You've got to be kidding me," I say.

"What?" he says, a bemused expression on his face.

"You can't say something like that and then just leave."

"I can't?" he says, smiling.

"No, you can't," I say. I feel like we're having a moment here. This is the moment that I've been building up to; this is the moment in every eighties teen movie where we'd kiss, then he'd fall madly in love with me and stand on my stoop with a boom box over his head blasting my favorite song that expressed perfectly exactly how he felt about me, which, of course, would be him being as in love with me as I was with him. That's why, of course, I flubbed it. "Kiss me before it's too late."

"Huh?"

"Kiss me before it's too late," I say again, but this time it sounds a little sad. Not sad-weepy, but sad-pathetic. I give my head a good shake and sit there quietly, holding my breath waiting to hear his response.

"I don't know if this is a good idea, Ri —"

"I don't care. If you don't do it now, it'll never happen," I say.

"I don't . . . I mean, what happens if it changes things? I think our friendship is really important and I don't want anything to change that."

"If you don't do it now, I will never have the guts to bring it up again," I explain. "I'll always be thinking about how the first time I asked you to kiss me, you said no, and I'll never be able to look you in the eyes again if I have to keep remembering it, so you either kiss me now or never."

He looks upset. I don't care.

We're both standing on the sidewalk. There isn't anyone near us. There isn't a lot of noise. It's a bright night, though — there must be a lot of midtown glow flowing uptown. He stands in front of me and bends his head just a little, his lips on mine.

And it's all wrong.

He leans back, a relieved look crossing his face.

"Wait," I say, and put my hands on either side of his face, drawing it closer to mine. I kiss him gently, and then again, and again, and again.

I feel everything for a moment. How close I'm standing to him, how far apart we are . . .

And then my brain clicks on. My hand is in his hair, I pull it down to his shoulders, I've always liked his shoulders. I tilt my head so our noses aren't bumping against each other. I lean back a little so my bazongas aren't pressed up against his chest. I thank God that I brushed my teeth before coming downstairs. I fidget in my shoes a little as his mouth opens against mine. I make this weird little noise that I make to show the guy I'm kissing that I like what he's doing. . . .

As quickly as it all began, it ends.

He steps back. Actually, he takes a big step back, his hands on my shoulders so I can't take the step with him, and he looks scared. I can't tell if I should be offended or not so I just rest my fingers against my lips and wait. He'll say something.

This was the thing I've been dreaming about for months, years, really. . . . But I don't feel anything more than when I kissed Timothy. I feel void. I feel scattered. I feel like it was a big . . .

"That was good," he says.

I begin to smile.

". . . I think that was a mistake," he finishes, and my smile breaks.

"Why? Because you liked it?" I asked. My voice sounds husky — like I'm trying to be sexy. This is me, this is what I do. This is Riley. Riley with all the other boys — the flirt, the tease, the plus-size (whatever) seductress. But I know something is wrong because this isn't how it's supposed to be with D. With D, it's supposed to be sweet, romantic, slow, life-changing.

"Yes," he says simply, looking at me.

There is a moment where you know something bad is going to come out of your mouth and you have a split second to turn around and walk away before you do something you can never undo. Instead, because I'm hurt by what he's saying (and everything he isn't saying), I stand my ground and smile, flick my hip out a little, and say, "I can think of a few other things you might like."

He looks pissed, but I can't tell if it's because he's reacting to my words or because I'm saying them to begin with.

"Riley," he says, and I feel a lecture coming on, so I just sigh and tell him to forget it. To go home, it was all a dream (la, la) and that he would forget about it come morning (la, la). He warns that we'll "talk about this soon."

Not if I can help it.

I walk inside and watch as he walks away.

I go to bed, again, replaying the kiss in my head that has already faded to absolutely nothing. It's gone before I even had a chance to really think about it. But what's left is the moments afterward. The way I treated him, the way he treated me, and how I reacted to it. And I realize, perhaps for the first time in the history of knowing D, that I might not be in love with him after all. I don't even know what to do with that, so I'm not going to think about it.

It was probably just the timing, or the situation. Perhaps it was the setting. The street in front of my building is not the most romantic setting. I should be happy and elated, actually.

He finally kissed me. Why am I so unhappy?

Dear Aaron,

I hope you like red wine!

This is a bottle from my father's cellar — it's very, very dusty — and we both know what that means! Very, very expensive.

I hope this makes the long, strenuous hours that you work as a lawyer more enjoyable. Perhaps, during one of those long hours, you could reply to my letter?

Cheers, *Riley Swain*

Aaron Tremaine, Esq.
Swain Corporate Headquarters
Legal Department
1020 Park Avenue | 13th Floor
New York, NY 10001

Dear Aaron,

I felt like we were growing quite close, so I'm sure you understand why I'm a little disappointed that I didn't hear from you personally. I do understand that you are "very busy" and I appreciated the handwritten note that your secretary sent by messenger to the house. Mary Beth has very nice handwriting.

Unfortunately, I am still scheduled to leave for New Horizons in just a few hours. Have you found any evidence at all to use against Elizabeth Butler? Would it help to know that she once threatened me? Her story is that I did "something" to her hair dryer. My story is that she's psychotic and über-obsessive about her hair. I have several people who can corroborate this story with me: Ricardo (her hairdresser), several of the household staff who heard her threaten me on April 3rd at 6:52 A.M., and my best friend, Michael D. Hammond III, who had just arrived with my venti skim latte (those are very good — you should have Mary Beth pick you up one) as we were about to leave for our yoga class.

I've attached an affidavit from Michael D. Hammond III regarding the incident in question.

I realize that lawyers are very, very important people (otherwise, why would there be so many jokes about them?) but I'd appreciate it if you could look into this matter directly.

Sincerely,

Riley Swain

Riley Swain

Encl: Affidavit M. D. Hammond III; Picture of Elizabeth Butler after the "hair dryer" incident; Picture of Elizabeth Butler after her bath (really, can you believe she has the gall to suggest I need fat camp?)

STEP INTO THE KILL ZONE

The car is coming to pick me up and take me to the train station in five minutes. The porter will be loading my bags in the back of the Lincoln, or whatever they are driving these days. I'll leave here alone.

It's raining. There are too many obvious references to make here, but let's just say that it's gross out and I am happier for it. I couldn't imagine leaving NYC on the most beautiful spring day ever. Plus, I know that the rain will keep Elizabitch inside with her frizzy, overly processed hair. She gets twitchy whenever she even hears it is *going* to rain. So she stands just inside the double doors while the doorman offers her an umbrella, and she just crinkles up her face and shakes her head, fiddling with her hair in a nervous birdlike way.

Elizabitch didn't start out as an evil bitch. I mean, she seemed nice enough the first time I met her, but since then all of my dad's free time (all twenty-two minutes a week) have revolved around Elizabitch and their wedding plans. It's hard to dislike her completely. . . . She is a nervous wreck of a woman. She comes from a good family (so say the private investigators — kidding), but her hands shake a little when she talks to strangers so she is always clasping them together or fidgeting with her hair. Dad says that's because she gets nervous.

When I asked him if he'd like me to set him up with someone who wasn't a twitcher (I mean really, he made me get rid of my Chihuahua because she kept getting so nervous she'd pee on the Persian rug — shouldn't I have the same option with Elizabitch?), he yelled at me. He had never yelled at me before, and the first time he did it, he did it right in front of Elizabitch and she had the nerve to be angry with me and pout at my father.

Now whenever I do anything she doesn't like, she goes and tattles to my father about my behavior or my "mean-heartedness." Which is really overdoing it.

My dad is under one of those huge navy blue umbrellas, and he has his arm around my shoulders. It is one of the rare times that I see him without his newspaper or his BlackBerry. I can see he is itching to pull it out and get a quick fix. Like a crack addict. I can feel it buzzing inside his jacket pocket when I stand close enough. It must be driving him insane — he has this weird, slightly disassociated look on his face.

Or it might've been that he just didn't care that I was leaving.

"You ready to go, tiger?" he says, smiling somewhere over my head. He gives me a tight squeeze, knocking me a little off-kilter. I refuse to look at him because I know that if I do, I'd beg him not to send me away. Worse — he may make me go anyway.

Elizabitch first talked with my dad about the New Horizons place and then he talked about it with me. Saying how *he* thought it was a great idea and how *he* was wondering if I'd want to go. He seemed really uncomfortable and then I felt really uncomfortable — and to put us both out of our misery I just said yes so he would go away. Thinking that he couldn't *really* be serious. He never seemed to care about how I looked or what I did. It had to be Elizabitch. I could smell her evilness all over this.

So what could I say at this point? "Um . . . Dad — I'd rather be fat and in Manhattan (even if my new stepmother looks like she's about to pull all her hair slowly out of her head while you're checking your BlackBerry) than go out in the middle of nowhere with a bunch of fat geeks"? Not so much.

"Yeah, I'm ready!"

He gives me another squeeze and shifts the box back into both arms before carrying it over to the truck.

"You'll have a fabulous time!"

I turn around and Elizabitch is standing on the stoop to our building. The rain has stopped. When my father notices, he smiles at her and closes the umbrella. She's wearing some pastel-yellow suit that washes her out completely. What I wouldn't do if I could just have five minutes with her wardrobe and stylist. What does my father see in her?

41

"Thanks, Elizabeth," I say, smiling as wide as I can. I can see her bright eyes. She thinks she's won! "By the way, I wouldn't use that hair iron of yours — I just saw a special report on CNN that said those things can suddenly short and burst into flames."

Her eyes narrow in suspicion and her hands begin to shake as she walks back in, slamming the door behind her. But I know that she won't be using that hair iron again.

Elizabitch — 1, Riley — 1.

"Riley," Dad says from behind me. I turn around and he's giving me that sad, tired look again.

"Sorry, Dad. I was just kidding."

He just sighs. I hate when he sighs like that.

"You really have to show her a little respect," he says.

"I do show her a little. Very little," I mumble.

"And stop writing to Aaron. He's not your personal confidante. He's the head of the company's legal department — do you know how many billable hours it takes to convince him that Elizabeth isn't trying to perpetrate some sort of crime?"

So much for lawyer-client confidentiality.

"Dad, really — I don't have to . . ."

But Dad doesn't hear me. Nothing unusual there. He's looking over my shoulder. "Mr. Hammond." He smiles, stepping around me, holding out his arm. The blood drains from my face as I turn around to face D. Please God, don't let my dad say anything embarrassing while D is here.

"Hello, Mr. Swain," D says, shaking Dad's hand. Dad grimaces a little at D's overenthusiastic grip.

"Here to see my little girl off?"

"Yes, sir," D says, giving me an eyebrow arch. D thinks my entire family is going to this really upscale spa in upstate New York, to bond before Dad and Elizabitch's wedding. It took me weeks to find an appropriate venue in the general direction of New Horizons that I could pass off as the place I was going to. He also thinks my dad is one of those eccentric rich guys who can't be trusted to say anything coherent. I'm not sure where he got that idea. I roll my eyes behind my dad's back and make "crazy man" gestures.

"Well, that's nice of you. She's very lucky to have such supportive friends." Dad turns around and looks at me, shooting me a confused look as I morph the "crazy man" gesture into a scratching-my-temple gesture.

"Huh?" D says, but I step in between them and give my dad the embarrassed-daughter look that makes him laugh and tell us "he'll leave us to our business." He heads back inside to give us some space.

"Aren't they going with you?" D asks, his face all scrunched up as he looks at where my dad just entered the house. There is one thing about D that you should know. He's an obsessive truth-teller. Obsessive. I think it all stems from some weird thing between his parents (aren't all of our flaws just a result of some weird thing with our parents?) but ever since I met him, he's never lied to me, not once. Not even when I really, really wanted him to.

Once, when I told a little white lie to him and he found out about it, it was this huge deal. And he made me swear to never lie to him again. I swore, of course, he was my best friend, of course I'd never lie to him again. . . .

But here I am, in the middle of a lie (once again) that is getting bigger and bigger. And while I'm not sure where that kiss left us . . . I can't lose my best friend and the first boy I ever thought I loved all in one swoop.

And you might be wondering why I lied to begin with.

You don't tell the boy you think you love (even if he *is* your best friend) that your dad is sending you to fat camp. You just don't. No matter how close you are. There are some things you keep to yourself.

RILEY'S LIST OF THINGS TO KEEP TO YOURSELF
1. Your parents are sending you to fat camp.
2. You're addicted to reading *Gossip Girl.*
3. You once ate a whole gallon of vanilla ice cream by yourself.

"Um, Dad had a last-minute scheduled meeting — so I'm heading up now and he and Elizabitc — Elizabeth will be up tomorrow morning."

He seems to accept this. His brow smooths and he smiles.

"At least you won't have to ride up with the both of them." But then his brow seems to crease again. "Um, Riley? About last night."

"Aren't you popular?" I hear coming from down the sidewalk.

"Oh, look, there is Marty Diggons's girl," Dad says, smiling from the doorway, walking back toward us (*MERDE!*).

If I have any blood left in my body it is now officially pooled around my toes and the lack of circulation has left my brain without the ability to process the fact that Marley Diggons is standing in front of my building, mere hours after I kissed the boy-she-is-crushing-on, in front of the boy-that-I-will-always-love-who-doesn't-know-I'm-going-to-fat-camp.

Why do these things happen to me?

"Good morning, Mr. Swain," Marley says, waving. Dad waves back. I'm going to vomit. She's wearing yellow (and yellow doesn't wash Marley out). She's always said yellow was her power color, ever since Edward Sullivan told her she looked pretty in her yellow Sunday dress in the third grade. She wears yellow when she has a fight to win.

She's here to ruin me.

"Marley, how nice of you to see me off to Dahlia's. I thought you had therapy every Saturday morning, and yet here you are!"

I hear her grind her teeth. D looks like he just wants to step back and get himself out of the kill zone. And that's when my father steps right into the kill zone. Clueless as usual.

45

"How's your dad, Marley?"

"Oh, he's fine, Mr. Swain. Asked about Riley just this morning, actually, so I thought I'd stop by."

"That's very nice of you. Well," he says, turning to me, "I'll let you say good-bye to your little friends in peace. We'll miss you. But we'll see you soon, OK? Call me if you need anything."

"Yeah, sure, Dad. Love you."

He pats me on the head and says good-bye to Marley and D.

"Wow, all that for one day? I thought *my* parents were clingy," D says, chuckling.

"Yeah," I agree, looking at Marley, who has a fire suddenly ignite behind her eyes. I don't want to say that Marley is dumb. But she's got these huge tits (fake), a blond little tuft of hair on her head (fake), and this little pert nose (fake) and this perfectly shaped ass (fake), and the best wardrobe that Daddy can afford (real) — all usually topped off with a blank look (real). So whenever she is having an actual thought, like an honest-to-goodness spark of brain activity, her eyes light up and she looks . . . well, sort of like she's constipated.

She looks pretty backed up at the moment.

I need to get out of here and I can't let them leave together.

DAMAGE CONTROL 101: NEVER LEAVE A GIRL WITH INFORMATION ALONE WITH THE BOY YOU LOVE.

"Well, D, thanks for coming. I appreciate you pulling your-self out of bed before noon," I say, balancing on my toes to give him a hug. I give him an extra squeeze so my boobs press against his chest — and suddenly I realize that whatever he wanted to say about last night, about our kiss, would be lost for now. Which I'm relieved about. Whatever he has to say, I'm not sure I want to hear it yet.

"Bye, Riley," Marley says, spreading her arms to give me a hug. Ew.

"Actually, why don't I drop you off — we're on our way down-town anyway," I say, holding the car open so she can scoot in.

"Well," she says, looking over at D expectantly, but D isn't paying attention or is ignoring her. I'm not sure. Could his behav-ior have to do with a certain lip-on-lip action? Oh my God.

She definitely won't be staying with him alone now anyway.

"Come on, Marley, stop shuffling your feet — D has stuff to do and can't spend all morning babysitting you." Sometimes honesty is not only the best policy but it's also embarrassing as hell. Marley turns bright red, D does his best to cover his smile, and I smirk. Marley gets into the car and scoots to the far side and I get in after her with a small wave in D's direction.

As the cab pulls away, I have my eyes on him. He has his hands tucked into his back pockets, his shades over his eyes. He looks hung over. He looks hot as hell. Two weeks, that's all, and then I'll be back in Manhattan. Back with my friends.

"I know where you're going."

Speaking of *friends*.

"Not exactly surprising, Marley," I say, rolling my eyes at her and grabbing my bag to look for a pack of gum. "Everyone knows where I'm going."

"No, I know where you are *really* going."

I pause for half a second in my search before I recall myself enough to laugh. But it sounds fake to my ears and I wonder what she knows and how she found out. What she said last night at the party makes me wonder . . . perhaps I didn't cover this far enough.

I steady my eyes on the passing sidewalk in an attempt to keep my stomach from flip-flopping, but the garbage cans, dogs being walked, doorman buildings, and the random church flying by my window at twenty miles an hour are not settling anything. Instead I stare straight forward, at my nail beds. I need a manicure.

"I'm going to Dahlia's Day Spa to relax a little during break and bond with the family," I say, abandoning my nails and finally finding the gum. I grab a stick and pop it in my mouth. After a few chews, I look at her, raising my eyebrows and putting on my most haute attitude. If nothing else, I need to bitch my way out of this one.

GIRL FIGHT 101: WHEN IN DOUBT, RELY ON ATTITUDE.

"Oh?" she says, pulling out her cell phone. "What's the name of the place you're staying at again?"

"Dahlia's, Marley. Really, if your memory is so bad, I hope you're not depending on your SATs to get you into any good schools. You'll forget how to fill in those little circle thingies . . . and then where will you be?"

"Buying my way into Columbia, same as you, I suspect."

The best part is, this entire conversation is said in these sweet dulcet tones. *Best* enemies, remember? Nothing but jokes and lighthearted banter. If anyone had overheard us speaking but didn't hear what we were saying, they'd assume we were having a sweet BFF chat. Ah, girl-speak.

"Look, call them and check, if you must," I say, pulling out my cherry lip gloss.

She looks at me for a moment, trying to decide if she should call my bluff or not, and at the last minute dials 411 and when she is connected to Dahlia's spa, she tells the receptionist that her BFF is scheduled to stay there for some time and she wants to join her but isn't sure what day I am leaving (and at this point even I have to admit that her acting is somewhat impressive), could she confirm my departure date?

"Are you sure?" she says, blinking into the phone. I know exactly what she is hearing. The receptionist is telling her that I am confirmed to depart the spa on Friday, just shy of one week from today.

ALIBI 101: IF YOU'RE GOING TO GO THROUGH ALL THE TROUBLE OF FINDING A FOUR-STAR SPA TO LIE TO YOUR FRIENDS ABOUT WHEN YOU'RE REALLY STAYING AT A NEARBY FAT CAMP, THE LEAST YOU SHOULD DO IS BOOK A STAY THERE IN CASE ANY OF YOUR "FRIENDS" FEELS THE NEED TO CONFIRM YOUR ATTENDANCE.

Marley is such an amateur.

Although at $1,200 per day, booking a stay at a spa that I wouldn't even be attending is a risk. I mean, eventually I'll have to explain the expenditure to my father, and when I made the reservation two weeks ago I didn't even know if it would be necessary, but it obviously is and since my dad is set on ruining my life, the least he can do is pay to protect my reputation.

I look out the window at the passing awnings with the numbers written on their faces. We are only a block away from Marley's apartment building, thank God. Another minute and I am in the clear.

"They said you had a reservation booked there until next Friday."

"Really, Marley, do we need to have this conversation again? Exactly where do you think I'm going? What else *is* there in upstate NY?" I laugh like she's stupid and for a moment she looks completely unsure of herself and I feel like I've won.

"I can't wait to tell D that you'll be coming with us to Mexico, then." She smiles triumphantly at me.

I'M SERIOUSLY SCREWED

I take a deep breath. The girl is really thick. Another example of rich people inbreeding.

"Marley, we've already been through this. . . ."

"Riley, your reservation is for one week. If that's what your reservation is for and that's where you really are going to be," Marley says as the car slows to a halt, "then you'll be home in time to go on the trip with all of us. Especially as we're not leaving until Sunday."

"Um . . ."

"I'm so glad," she says, all smiles now. She is practically batting her eyelashes (fake). "I was worried that I wouldn't really have anyone to talk to on the trip."

I still don't know what to say. I can't believe I was so stupid. I did all the prep work and I missed it by one day. One day! How can I fix this? How can I cover this up without —

"I was telling D that I would be really lonely without you there, and he was gallant enough to promise to stick by my side the entire time if necessary."

I bet.

She opens the door and has a foot out before she glances back at me over her shoulder. "I'm so glad you're coming, Riley. D and I would've really missed you" (BITCH) "and now you'll get to see my brand-new bikini!" (Double BITCH)

I sit numbly in the backseat, nodding like an asshole, while she slams the door shut and prances her size-2 body (fake) up the walk to her building. Before I even have time to recover, before I even make it to the train station, I have a text from D:

M SAYZ UR GNG ON TRP. :> WE ND 2 TLK SN, K?

I flop over in the backseat and wish for a fast and easy death. The love of my life is going to Mexico with my best enemy, everyone else thinks I am going to Dahlia's Day Spa with my parents, and now that I am going to be on the trip, and . . . and I am headed to fat camp. Lies, lies, lies.

Swell.

I HATE NATURE, NATURE STINKS

Nature smells funny. I'm trying to get it into my head that this is called fresh air and it's the trees and all that, but honestly, it smells funny. I want to hold my nose, but I look around and nobody else is holding their nose, which makes me wonder if it's all in my head. But I swear, nature smells funny. Kind of like . . . dog pee. Or something rotting.

"It's not you."

I look up and there is a boy, a very odd-looking boy, standing in front of me. In the city, everyone knows you don't stare at odd-looking boys. I stare off into the distance right above his shoulder so he doesn't feel like it's really an invitation to interact. He doesn't notice and settles onto the bench right next to me.

I glance at him out of the corner of my eye and he's got his hair growing in a sort of weird floppy Mohawk. I think he's wearing nail polish and he's wearing bracelets that I suppose are meant to cover up the tattoos on the underside of his wrists, which I can see even if I can't tell what the tattoo is of. When he smiles, his eyes scrunch up a little (he's wearing eyeliner) and he looks a bit like Pete Wentz.

I slip my hand into my bag and finger my pepper spray. The kid doesn't even notice; he actually slides in closer until I can feel my thighs bump against his a little. Personal space?

"What's not me?" I ask him.

He points a hand up to the beautiful trees I'm sitting under. Remember, almost everything is context. If you can sit among beautiful things, you will appear more beautiful (unless it's girls — when you sit amid beautiful girls, you shouldn't expect much). I saw these trees off to the side of the rail station where I was supposed to call and wait for my ride.

I was only two hours late (I missed the first train, having forgotten my cell in the car and made it turn around and come back for me) and by the time I called the school, the secretary seemed pissed off — but that might just be because she lives in upstate NY and is a secretary. Seriously, I'd be pissed off too.

People who know me know I have a habit of losing my cell phone. I'm on my seventh one this year, and Dad told me that if I lost this one, that was it. I was done and he wasn't going to replace it, so I've been wayyyy more careful with this one. Whenever I lose it, I even look for it before thinking about buying a new one.

Despite having to take a later train, I am in a pretty good

mood, so I let the secretary's evilness slide (really, who is paying whom here?) and figure I'll wait the "fifteen to twenty" minutes for my ride (seriously, what — they've never heard of cabs before?) under these trees that have these gorgeous white flowers. It feels very upstate NY and, I figure, do as the locals do.

"It's the trees," the boy beside me says.

"What's the trees?"

He looks at me like I may be stupid. Why is everyone looking at me like this lately? I did freakin' fab on my PSATs! I'm in honor classes!

"You don't smell that?" he asks.

"Smell what? I smell . . ." I take a big whiff and scrunch up. I smell something. But am I smelling the same thing he's smelling? He's looking at me funny. I look at him funny back.

"It smells bad. Like cat piss."

"Yes!" I say before I can stop myself.

"It's the trees."

"The trees smell like cat piss?" I look him over, trying to decide if he's crazy — actually, I glance around to see how many people are around who could save me if he decides to try pulling me into the woods to murder me. Not that I think he could. I think he's barely my height, perhaps even shorter. But he looks like he's got some muscles under the loose blue shirt he's wearing with his baggy jeans. And he's definitely wearing nail polish. This is so Midwest punk. God save me from upstate NY.

"Yeah, it's the pollen. I'm surprised you can't smell it," he says, smiling at me in a way that makes me flush a little. He did something weird to his eyebrows, looks like he shaved a line into them. For a second I feel like smiling back until I realize that he's the exact opposite of D in every way imaginable — except maybe the shoulders. This kid . . . er, guy . . . has great shoulders.

"I can smell it," I say, feeling a little tense. "I just thought it was —"

"Cat piss?"

"I'm sorry," I say, "I haven't spent a lot of time smelling cat piss, so I'll have to take your word for it."

"What did you think it smelled like? Eau de toilette?" I think he's making fun of me, probably because he's smiling (great smile), but I can't be sure.

"Actually, I thought it was just nature."

"Nature?"

"Yes," I say, waving my hands around — pointing at grass, leaves, smelly trees, air. "Nature?"

"You think nature smells like cat piss?"

"I think nature in upstate NY smells like cat piss, yes. Nature in Manhattan smells like homeless dudes and dog piss."

And then he starts laughing. Oh boy. I feel this weird warm flush when he laughs. I look away, start searching my bag for my phone, suddenly nervous.

"No, no, sorry. I'm not laughing at you," he says, pulling my hand away from my bag and patting it with his right hand. Is he seriously holding my hand? Do they have no sense of personal boundaries up here?

"Actually," I say, yanking my hand back, "I'd love to stay and chat but I'm waiting for a ride."

I stand up and begin to walk away.

"I'm your ride," he says, coming up behind me.

I turn. "Are you flirting with me? I mean, is this the way guys pick up girls in upstate New York?"

He looks at me and quirks a half smile. He smiles too much.

"Look, you're cute . . ." I start, to which he raises his eyebrows. "I'm not even so much into guys who wear nail polish. And I like tall guys. With dark hair. And kimonos. But you've got something, I can admit that. But *this* probably isn't going to happen."

He's still smiling. A full smile. I want to smack him.

"What?" I snap.

"Kimonos?"

"I'm thinking of someone in particular," I say, tucking my hair behind my left ear. Nervous habit. I watch as he turns around and walks back to the bench under the smelly trees and picks up my bag.

"I'm your ride. To New Horizons. I assume you're Riley. They told me that I'd find you here," he says.

I feel my face flush. I'm beet red — of course he knew it was me because there are only so many fat chicks at the station.

Jesus, he could've been a little circumspect about it. What if I wasn't Riley? Or does he just go around corralling all the fat girls who happen to meander into the area? I'm starting to feel like I should be offended.

"Look, how do you know I'm Riley? I could be anyone. I could be Joanne."

"You're not Joanne," he says, putting the bags down between us and rubbing his chin. "Definitely a Riley. You have a certain sophistication about you — very New York City. Something about your eyes. They're very honest."

"Really?"

"No. But not a lot of people stop at this station, you're alone, you appeared to be waiting for someone. I'm here to pick up someone. You think *nature* smells. . . . Plus, they gave me your picture that came with your application."

Picture?

He pulls a piece of paper out of his back pocket, unfolds it, and shows it to me. It's a photocopy of my sophomore-year picture. Not the worst picture of me, but it could've been better. I liked my hair that way, at least.

"Oh," I say, reaching out for the picture. He pulls it out of my reach, shakes his head at me, and folds it up carefully before putting it back into his pocket.

"You're not going to do weird, perverted things with that later, are you?" I ask.

"Definitely," he says, picking up my bag again and motioning to the left where a minivan is parked. We walk toward it together, neither of us moving very fast. "I've already got a bath running, scented candles, and some classical music. It's going to be very sensual. I'd actually like to get back to it sooner rather than later. . . ."

He holds the door open for me, and I slide into the seat.

After a few moments he's climbing into the driver's seat — if anyone doesn't belong behind the wheel of a minivan (and I mean, besides me . . . I wouldn't be caught dead driving a minivan), it's this guy. I want to say something as he starts the car. I'm not used to not knowing what to say. I always know what to say. I'm fabulous[1], dammit!

"I don't even know your name," I finally spit out.

"I know. Romantic, isn't it?"

I pause for a moment, but he doesn't continue. "Seriously, aren't you going to tell me your name?"

"How about this — you get to ask me three questions," he says, his eyes flicking over to meet mine. I turn to face the road. Someone should be watching where we are going. Goodness, I can't even remember the last time I was in the front seat of a vehicle. "And I'll get to ask you three questions."

---

1. I know I keep throwing the word *fabulous* around — and it's a word that should be used with care. Fabulous, in Riley-speak, is more than just what you wear, or who does your hair. Those things are obviously important, but fabulous is the way you hold yourself, the way you inspire others to treat you. You can be a fabulous circus clown. You can be an unfabulous heir to a fortune (Elizabitch). It's all about the attitude. More on this later.

"Deep, for a driver."

"Perhaps," he says, raising his eyebrows.

"Fine. What's your name? Why nail polish? And when did you lose your virginity?"

He gasp-laughs and I feel better about myself, like he's finally feeling as off-kilter as I am. And I suspect that he'll never answer the last one, if he's even straight. (Although I figure he is. I mean, it's just . . . well, I don't think a gay boy would ever look at me quite the way this boy is looking at me. Is that weird to say?)

"Eric. I like it. Fifteen, with my girlfriend who was older, wiser, and more experienced but loved me enough to deal with the fact that I didn't know what the hell I was doing. But then again, who could blame her? I'm irresistible."

"Wow . . ."

"My turn," he starts.

"Wait! 'I like it.' That's not a real answer," I say, turning in my seat a little to face him.

"Well, I don't know. I think it looks good. I like it. Why not?"

I don't say anything. Put that way, it makes more sense than any reason I can come up with not to do it. I let it go.

"OK," he starts again. "What do you have in your bag, what's the weirdest thing you've ever done with a stranger, and . . . how do you like to be kissed?"

We are driving along a two-lane street that doesn't even have sidewalks. In fact, it seems like nature is bumping right up against the side of the road. It's like this: grass, asphalt, grass . . . and these big trees with big green leaves are branched over the street like a canopy. The sun peeks through, leaving a sunshine pattern on the roadway before us. Every once in a while there is a small house set off the road a little, usually with a crappy-looking car in the driveway and a really sad, mangy-looking dog out front. I wonder if the dog is a requirement if you live in upstate NY; it seems like every house has one.

I open the window and let the wind mess my hair up. Nature. How lovely.

"Let's see, I have my wallet, my Starbucks card that's empty. A makeup kit with two tampons and a condom that I've had since freshman year — the condom, not the tampons. Breath mints. Cherry lip gloss. My cell. A digital recorder. Two pens," I say, rifling through my bag. "And a Hello Kitty notebook."

"Hello Kitty?"

"Nail polish?"

"Touché."

"*This* is probably the weirdest thing I've ever done with a stranger. And well."

"Well what?"

"I like to be kissed well."

"Cop-out."

"Nothing too wet. Lots of lips. Let it evolve naturally. Hands in the hair."

"Nice," he says. Eric slows down and signals left, before we start pulling into a long drive, with NEW HORIZONS written on an arch above us. The campus looks like the New-England-style college campuses you are always seeing in movies. It's clean and manicured; there are trees everywhere and big brick buildings with pillars that are trying to look important. I'm starting to feel nervous so I finger the fringe on my purse.

"Do you work at this place?"

"I'm sorry, but you are over your three-question allotment."

"You're serious?"

"As a heart attack," he says and smiles again. I turn to look out the window so he can't see that I'm smiling back. He pulls us up in front of one of the larger brick buildings and I'm itching to pull out my New Horizons map to see which building this is, but that is *so* tourist. In less than five minutes, Eric has my bags out of the car and on the stoop (the building gets larger and uglier up close) that he tells me is the Victoria Dormitory.

It sounds a lot nicer than it looks. I want to ask him another question, perhaps only to find out if I'll see him again while I'm here. Which would be nice. I mean, knowing someone. So I cry that I forgot a bag in the car (which I didn't). Instead, while I'm searching for this mysterious bag (and Eric is standing on the stoop looking adorably confused), I toss my cell phone in the backseat.

HINT: CONVENIENTLY MISPLACED CELL PHONES MAY NECESSITATE A CONVENIENTLY TIMED CALL BACK.

"Sorry," I say, shrugging. "I don't know what I'm thinking. I must've decided not to take that bag. I must just be really nervous." I smile a big, charming Riley smile.

"You'll be fine, Riley with the Hello Kitty notebook," he says, taking my hand and shaking it.

"I'm sure I will," I say, hoping to be a bit huffy about it. Like he should even question whether or not I would be OK. Instead he just laughs and gives my hand a little squeeze.

He starts walking back around the minivan and I yell after him, "Make sure you return that picture!"

"I'll take good care of her," he says, his hand up in the air in good-bye. He gets in the car as I pick up my bags and drag them inside. I hear him honk as the door shuts behind me with a resounding thud.

HOW TO GET OFF ON THE RIGHT FOOT

Let me get this straight, you simply got on the wrong train?" The program director, Gwendolyn Hotra, looks like everything you'd expect the head honcho of a fat-girl program to look like: a Pilates-loving Martha Stewart. Big. Blond. Hair. Everywhere. Probably vanilla-scented too — but I'd have to get a bit closer, and I'd rather not.

"That's right," I say.

"Why didn't you call?" That's my dad. Or rather, his voice coming from the speaker phone. Even the threat that his only daughter had been kidnapped or had gone missing wasn't enough to get him away from his weekly poker game.

"She never thinks, Richard. I've been telling you this for months." Elizabitch. Conference calls suck.

When I walked into the Victoria, within five minutes I was being whisked away to the magical land of the program director's office. Of course I had to walk by the troll first (secretary), and only to be subjected to the spite of a program director who probably hasn't sworn in the past decade.

"I told you, my cell phone was stolen."

"Stolen? Or did you forget it in the car again?" (Dad)

Someone snorts. (Elizabitch)

"Either way, I think there will have to be some sort of pun-ishment for this." (Program director) "We cannot just leave this issue unaddressed. There were a lot of people inconve-nienced because of . . ." She looks over at me.

"Because of her irresponsible and completely self-centered behavior." (Elizabitch again)

"Right." (Dad, with a long-suffering sigh)

Suddenly I'm just really tired of trying to explain the entire situation. It isn't such a big deal in NYC to be an hour late. People understand things like traffic and catching the wrong train. But I can tell when I'm outnumbered. I've been surrounded. Their aims are trained. Waiting. To. Pull. The. Trigger.

If I had my phone, which I think Eric might have stolen since he hasn't come to return it to me, I'd call a cab (if they had cabs . . .) and I'd be out of here.

"I think a demerit is in order," Mrs. Hotra says. "We work on a demerit system here at New Horizons. A demerit or partial demerit is given for an infraction against program rules or for inappropriate behavior. We feel like this allows the girls to see a direct result of their actions."

Kaboom!

"While I believe this behavior merits one demerit, every girl at New Horizons gets two demerits before she has some privilege taken away, and after three demerits she is sent home. . . . It's all in the handbook," she finishes off, smoothing the front of her pale blue suit that she probably bought at JCPenney.

"I think that sounds entirely reasonable."

"If not more."

Mrs. Hotra turns to me. "Do you have anything you'd like to add, Ms. Swain?"

I consider telling her where she can stick her demerit. But Dad's still on the phone, it's my first night here, and I'll admit that I could've handled my MIA a little better. Plus, the PD could totally break every bone in my body without breaking a sweat. So I just say, "I'd like to be shown to my room, please."

I can tell from the look on the PD's face that she was expecting something more. An apology? A full confession? Preferably in blood? Keep waiting, honey. I have nothing to prove to someone who has already decided — from the look on her face — that she hates my guts.

I tip my chin up.[2] I'm smart. I'm beautiful. And I'm more important than you. At the very least, tipping your head back helps keep tears from rolling down your cheeks.

Day 1: New Horizons — 1, Riley Swain — 0.

"You're excused, Ms. Swain. I believe that my son showed you where your dorm was. Someone will meet you to take you

---

2. Those wishing to learn how to be fabulous, please pay attention.

to your room. I expect to see you first thing Monday morning after Pilates."

"Your son?" I ask, halfway out the door already.

"Yes, Eric. My son. You are excused," she says before slamming the door in my face. I practically have to jump back to avoid getting my toes stubbed.

Summarily dismissed, ruined my fabulous exit, got a demerit, and am being stalked by the son of a fat-camp director. Life doesn't get better than this.

CASE OF THE CRAZY EX-GIRLFRIEND — TAKE ONE

Y ou must be Riley."

My first impression of Jennifer Sylvan is that she's too thin to be at a fat camp. I mean, she's not twiggy, but she's definitely an "after" picture. She's slightly round but wears her thick hair in a sharp bob around her chin. She's got some serious 1940s-hot-chick thing going on, or at least that's what she's trying for.

She introduces herself and explains that she attends New Horizons all year round, has since her freshman year, that it's a great place, great friends, the staff is so supportive — I tune out around here when she starts sounding like the brochure. Either she wrote it or she's been drinking the Kool-Aid. I think it freaks me out all the more because of how she looks. She looks like she's all about anarchy, but when she speaks she sounds very Connecticut. I wonder if this is a teen rebellion thing and for a moment think we could be great friends — especially if she hates her parents as much I hate mine.

"So you like it here?"

"Yeah," she says, giving me a funny look. Like, *Haven't you been listening to my spiel for the last forty-five minutes?*

"I guess it's not a bad place," I say. "I mean, anything is better than being with your parents."

"Actually," she starts, "I live locally and am a day student. Which is great, because I don't think I could stand to be away from my family for too long. We live about ten minutes away from here."

Jeez.

"But," she continues, "during the spring breaks I do extra volunteer work around campus, so I stay in the dorms because they are basically empty. Most of the students go home to spend time with their families."

"Oh, um, that's great," I say. I have absolutely nothing in common with this girl. Volunteer work? Family? Feh.

"So I hear that Eric Hotra gave you a ride here," she says, her voice über-casual.

"Um, yeah," I say. She stands in front of me in the hallway and I peek around. We're on the third floor of the Victoria Dormitory and the walls are made out of cinder blocks. They painted them this hideous blue color and stuck a strip of cork at the top so people can hang . . . ugh, is that a Backstreet Boys poster? Seriously, I'm in a foreign country.

Jennifer fishes in her pocket for the key to my new room. I'm so ready to fall over dead, not only because I traveled to hell and back but because I'm carrying what must be forty pounds of clothing on my back like a pack mule. Jennifer is just standing there, waiting for me to say something.

"He's really nice. A bit weird, but really nice," I say, hoping that will dislodge her from the front of my door.

"Who?"

"Eric."

"Oh?" she says, like she's surprised I even brought him up. I can see this girl having some sort of crush on him; he seems like he'd be her type. "How so?"

"Well, he's not really my type," I start. "But he's kinda cute — in a charming, punk boy type of way."

She doesn't say anything, but it doesn't matter. I'm beginning to warm up to the subject. "I mean, some guys you can tell you want them just by looking at them, you know? But I didn't feel that way with Eric."

"No?" she says. And if her voice sounded a little choked, I didn't notice it until later when I started thinking about it, my head buried under my pillow.

"But he has a way of saying things that make you feel good, like he likes you or wants to really know you. Plus he's got a great smile. But then again," I say, trying to round off the conversation, "I don't really know him that well. Just an initial impression."

"You're right," she says, and I turn around to smile at her. "You don't really know him."

Whoa. What?

"Huh?"

"I mean, he's nice enough," she says. "A really great friend. But he's charmed more girls here out of their pants than you can imagine."

"Really?" I ask. I'm a little more interested, but I can't tell if I'm faking it because I want to go to bed, or because I want to know more about Eric. I can imagine him as a flirt. And that flirt still has my phone!

"Yeah, basically everyone here has fallen for him at one point or another. He's a player. It doesn't hurt that he's the only guy on campus, or that he'd never get in trouble because of who his mother is."

"I've never seen a player wearing nail polish," I say helpfully. It's become painfully obvious that Jennifer Sylvan is madly in love with Eric Hotra. Fucking fabulous. Five minutes here and I'm already stepping hip-deep in mud.

"Yes. Well . . . I guess you're next. There aren't many options during the spring break anyway."

Erm. Thanks so much. Bitch.

"Yeah . . . well, good-bye, then," I say, smiling in a hopeful manner, turning the key in my door. And scurrying in and slamming the door shut. I'll worry about Jennifer tomorrow.

WHERE I AVOID SERIOUS (PHONE) CONVERSATION

THEBIGUN17: Hey, I got your email and I called, what's up? Why didn't you pick up your phone?

RILEDUP: It was stolen.

THEBIGUN17: Left it somewhere again?

RILEDUP: STOLEN.

THEBIGUN17: Right. Well, what's the big emergency?

RILEDUP: I kissed D.

THEBIGUN17: . . . <!>

RILEDUP: You can say that again.

THEBIGUN17: So . . . you're together now?

RILEDUP: I don't think I like him.

THEBIGUN17: . . . after all that? One kiss and you know?

RILEDUP: How much do you need?

THEBIGUN17: Are you sure?

RILEDUP: I'm not sure about ANYTHING. Except that he can't find out that I'm here.

THEBIGUN17: I thought we talked about this.

RILEDUP: Don't yell at me, I'm going to cry.

THEBIGUN17: What's your number in the room?

RILEDUP: There's a community phone down the hall.

THEBIGUN17: Community?

RILEDUP: Yeah, like we have to share it.

THEBIGUN17: . . . .

THEBIGUN17: Bail, come here instead — you can live in my closet. I'll sneak you bread crumbs and tepid water.

RILEDUP: Add in an hour of pilates and you just described my fabulous new life here.

THE POSSIBILITY HAS ARISEN THAT MY ROOMMATE COULD BE A KILLER

I was dreaming that I was playing Elizabeth Bennet from *Pride and Prejudice* and Colin Firth was confessing that he admired me greatly and was begging me to put him out of his misery and consent to becoming his wife. Of course, I was like, "Totally" — because I'm not nearly as stupid (or stuck-up) as Elizabeth Bennet. It's not every day that Colin Firth proposes. Hot, rich guy with a fabulous accent? SIGN ME UP.

Then he was telling me how hot I was and we were about to start making out when this weird buzzing sound started coming out of his mouth. And then I realized that the buzzing sounded a lot like an alarm clock and *poof* — Colin was gone. Elizabeth Bennet, cool as England, pretty clothes, and a twenty-inch waist? Gone.

I opened my eyes and went from a Colin Firth dream to a New Horizons nightmare. It was enough to make me cry.

There was a freckled girl sitting on her bed in the corner, her long frizzy hair covering most of her face, her shoulders hunched . . . ohhh, bad posture. That's a confidence killer. She was already dressed, just looking at me.

Um. OK. I'm rooming with a psycho.

What's that thing you're supposed to say to psychopaths so they don't murder you? God, I have no idea. What's the point of watching *CSI* and all those other stupid shows if you can't even remember what to do when faced with your own murderer?

"Good morning," psycho-sleep-watcher says.

"Good. Morning," I say slowly. Oh, that's it, you're supposed to remind them of your humanity. Like, remind them that you're human by talking about very human things. "I have to pee."

That surprised psycho-sleep-watcher. She blinked at me. "You're not going to pee in the bed, are you?"

"Um. No." She obviously doesn't know how much 600-count Egyptian cotton costs. Then again, all my sheets are crumpled at the foot of my bed because I hadn't made the bed correctly last night. Because I was so tired, I simply laid them across the mattress (Note: mattress was lumpy, exactly what you'd expect from a boarding school in upstate NY).

"Well, the bathroom is down the hall."

"WHAT?" I kick the covers off my right foot and jump into sitting position.

"The bathroom is down the hall."

I give her a sharp look. I know I am not going to like the answer to this next question, but I had to ask anyway. "Exactly how many people are expected to use this bathroom?"

"Just the girls in this wing."

I continue to stare. I need hard numbers.

"Eight."

"Eight!?"

"Well, usually it's more, but there are only eight girls on this floor during spring break."

EIGHT? I jump off the bed and stride straight toward my Gucci bag that I had tossed on the one bare desk the night before. Potential psycho-killer forgotten, I pull out my little Hello Kitty notebook and begin scribbling a note to Aaron.

"What are you doing?" fuzzy-haired-psycho-sleep-watcher asks.

"Documenting evidence for my lawyer. Don't leave this room, I'm going to need an affidavit from you."

"Saying what, exactly? That we use toilets?"

"Wait." I begin rummaging through my suitcases, which are stacked next to my desk, and pull out a small digital recorder. I walk over to my psycho-sleep-watcher/roommate and, after checking the batteries, press REC.

"Could you please state your name, age, and occupation for the court?" I ask, holding the recorder under her nose.

"Eh . . ."

"Please speak up, the entire jury will need to hear you."

"Samantha Owens, sixteen, student."

"And can you please repeat, for the record, what you just told me?" She looks at me and I nod toward the mic. "Remember to speak loudly and clearly."

She nods at me and says loudly and clearly, "You're not going to pee in the bed, are you?"

I snap off the mic as she cracks a smile. "This could be considered tampering with evidence."

She begins to laugh.

I sigh heavily and throw the mic down next to psycho-sleep . . . I mean, Samantha, and grab my towel, walking out of the room toward the COMMUNITY bathroom. Gross.

James Corwin
Northern New York District
Food and Drug Administration
5600 Fishers Lane
Rockville, NY 11093

Riley Swain
New Horizons
19 School House Road
Bangor, NY 19119

Dear Ms. Swain,

Thank you for sending us your recent report regarding New Horizons. Unfortunately, we are unable to follow up on your claim at this time. In general, the Food and Drug Administration is the regulating body for food and medical products (including adverse reactions to those products), vaccines, blood transfusions and donations, animal feed, veterinary products, cosmetics, and similar products sold online.

Below are agencies that are more appropriate to addressing your concerns:

"Poisoning" — I can only assume this is said tongue-in-cheek. If not, you should contact your local poison control center or hospital right away — although, by the time you receive this letter, you may have already expired.

Potential "hazardous chemicals" — the Department of Labor's Occupational Safety and Health Administration should have an office near Bangor.

That said, I'd like to add that food that is clearly done in bad taste (no pun intended) may appear to be poisonous or full of potentially hazardous ingredients when, really, it simply suffers from poor preparation.

Before we began couples counseling, I thought my wife was intentionally trying to poison me. As it turns out, it was completely unintentional.

Sincerely,

James Corwin

James Corwin

SPOTTED DOGS

After I brave a shower and a tooth-brushing in the skanky bathroom, Samantha tells me that it is time for breakfast. I stop myself from saying THANK GOD. I haven't had anything to eat since yesterday morning when I shoved half a bagel in my mouth before leaving. And perhaps I bought a Snickers bar on the train. But that was LONG gone, and now my stomach is empty.

We walk across the campus (which takes no more than four minutes; this is NOT a big campus — "campus" might be implying something too collegiate, big, or impressive. Let's just call it a lawn. Like, a backyard lawn).

We walk across a backyardlike lawn toward the "Caf" — which apparently is short for cafeteria. I am about to eat food out of a cafeteria. I think I'm going to retch.

Instead I get in line behind Samantha, who can't stop chattering the whole time about who this and that is, and how she'll be happy to show me around and did I see the library yet.

Yes, I've been here and conscious for approximately fourteen minutes and the first thing I went for was the *library*?

I am in a foreign country. A foreign country filled with geeks!

But since she is the only person I know (except for Jenny the Eric-Lover Girl, who is nowhere to be found, although if I did find her, I'm not sure if I would sit with her), I follow Samantha to a small table that has three other girls of various fatness sitting at it.

I look around me. The food is gross. The company is depressing. The room is cavernous and there are only maybe fifteen people in it. I am losing my appetite.

"Is this it?"

"What?" Samantha says, looking around trying to see what I am looking at.

"Is this everyone?"

"Um, a few people might've slept in."

Sleeping in was an option?

"But, yeah . . . there are a lot fewer people here during —"

"Spring break? Yeah, yeah, I know."

I sit down and the other girls say hello to Samantha but avoid looking at me, even when Samantha introduces them. There is one mousy-looking girl named Allie and a really short, really round girl who could totally use an eyebrow plucking named Julie.

I just roll my eyes and concentrate on the food in front of me. Something on this tray has to be edible.

I start mixing my low-fat "spotted dog" — which is, according to Samantha, a favorite here at New Horizons. It's a kind of rice pudding mixed with raisins. There are so many things wrong with this, I'm unsure of where to start explaining. . . . Let's just say I don't eat anything that looks like it's already been digested.

"I want a four-cheese omelet," I speak up.

There is at least one gasp.

"And . . . pancakes," says Allie, looking animated for the first time.

". . . and bacon."

"You should've gotten the fresh fruit with cottage cheese," Samantha pipes in. The killjoy.

Cottage cheese. I repeat: I do not like eating anything that looks like it's already been digested.

"I'll pass."

"Hey, ladies." Eric walks up to us. His blond hair spikes a little bit at the front. He is wearing dark green khaki shorts, skate-boarding sneakers, and a T-shirt that clings to his shoulders.

"Riley," Samantha says, elbowing me in the side.

"What?" I snap, looking up from Eric's abs. Everyone is watching me, including Eric. "I'm sorry, I was too busy undressing Eric with my eyes. What's going on?"

One of the girls, who is just settling into a seat diagonal from me, gasps, and I hear Samantha muffle a laugh behind her hand, but Eric — Eric just smiles.

"That's so freaking rude," says another girl standing at the table, with a tray in hand. She has a pug nose (I would've gotten some work done if that were my nose), a really bad perm, and her outfit . . . goodness, it looks like she couldn't find her way to the mall with a flashlight and a black American Express, but whatever.

"Don't worry about it, Tilly." (Really, what kind of name is Tilly?) "With a body like this, I expect as much." Eric leans back and begins to flex his arm muscles — posing for us until even Tilly has to laugh at the spectacle he is making. Tilly smiles at Eric like he's a god and sits down across the table from me. For a moment I've forgiven her for being absolutely heinous, but then she shoots me a double-dirty stare when Eric looks away from her. Whatever.

"Sometimes," Eric continues, "I don't brush my hair — just so I can give other guys a chance."

"Kind of you," I say, nodding.

"I thought so."

I didn't notice Jennifer approach until it was too late. I mean, it was bad enough to have been caught in that awkward conversation last night, but to be caught smiling at a potential player in front of the potential player's last major heartbreakee the very next day? I was scared to think of what the consequences would be.

"Hey, Jenny," Eric says, his smile faltering just for a second before it comes back as bright and shiny as ever. My eyes volley between his face and hers. His seems normal enough; hers is a mixture of sadness and pissed-offedness. Hmm. Did he sleep with her and then never call her again? Likely.

"Hi, Eric," she says, standing there for a really long, really awkward amount of time while Tilly pushes her chair close to Allie's, making room for Jenny next to her.

"Do you want to sit with us?"

I felt for sure she'd say no, but instead, she decides to sit down right next to me — so that we're both sitting across from Eric. Tilly is sitting on his right and shooting me the glares of death, either because I was flirting with Eric or because Jenny decided to grace ME with her presence instead of her. . . . I have no idea. I must've run over a little rat terrier in a former life or something.

"Eric —" Jennifer starts.

"Riley —" Eric starts, stopping and looking at Jennifer. "Sorry, what?"

"Um, nothing. Go ahead."

"Riley, I have your cell phone. I found it on the seat in the van." He takes it out of his pocket and places it on the table.

Tilly mumbles something that sounds like, "Probably the backseat." But before I can respond, Jennifer stands up short, knocking over her one-percent milk (gross) into what looks like cottage cheese (double gross) and a slice of fruit. (Is this really breakfast? No wonder they expect people to lose weight.)

The entire table watches as Jennifer picks up her tray, apologizes to Samantha, who sat on the other side of her, ignoring the fact that she got milk all over my tray and not Samantha's, and walks to the side of the room in a huff.

"What was that all about?" I ask, turning to the rest of the table.

Eric's eyes are on the back of Jennifer's head. "I'll be right back," he says, standing up and following in Jennifer's wake.

"Seriously, is there something I should know?" I ask the table. Everyone is looking down at their plates, except Tilly, who is still shooting me daggers.

"What?" I finally snap at her, hoping she'll back down.

"I don't know what you think you're doing with Eric," she says, "but I hope you know he's too good for you."

"Excuse me?" I screech.

"Tilly —" Samantha starts.

"He's been with Jenny for three years now, and no one — especially not a tramp like you — is going to stop that." She gets up with a huff that sounds like she's about to start crying, and follows Jenny out the door.

"What the hell?" I ask. Nobody says anything. Nobody even makes eye contact. Fine, if you can't beat them, join them. I grab my tray and get up from the table, walking away from the group. I'm only going to be here for two weeks. I don't need this drama. I don't even need to get involved. I have a life, a good life — a GREAT life back home — I don't need these people's backward-assed problems screwing with my real goals: getting home and back to the people who mean something.

I'm particularly disgusted with Samantha, who seemed really cool (OK, that might be pushing it a little) for about five seconds, but maybe it's something about the nature up here. Tilly is obviously insane. Jenny has some weird issue with Eric. Eric is probably a player who wears nail polish to throw girls off his sex-obsessed scent. The entire place is crazy and I've just about had enough.

I make my way out of the cafeteria and out into the public veranda when I hear someone calling my name. I know it's Eric, unless Tilly's voice dropped by half an octave. He's the only boy on campus.

I keep walking. I cross the grass in front of the Victoria Dorm and go around the building where there is a small grove of trees. I head toward them, hoping he'll just give up and leave me alone. God knows what'll happen if people see us speaking together. I'll probably be deemed slut of the west and burned at the stake at midnight. I refuse to be burned at the stake — at least not here, where I haven't done anything.

"Riley, wait up," he calls from behind me.

"Go away, Eric. There is absolutely nothing you can say to me that will make me stop!"

"You left your cell phone on the table. . . . I brought it out for you."

OK, well, I guess there is one thing he could say. I stop and let him catch up. He hands me my phone, which I flip open to note that I have thirteen missed calls. Ugh. I snap it shut, shoving it in my back pocket.

"That's probably why you're always losing it. When you sit down, it'll push up and out of your pocket," he says, pointing at my ass.

"Please stop looking at my butt. And please stop talking about my butt."

"Um," he says, his eyes wide. "I wasn't. I was talking about your cell phone."

"And please stop talking to me, period! I've only been here, like, five minutes and already half the girls hate my guts and think we had sex in your minivan. God knows why. I don't even like you that much." (He takes a step back.) "And you totally ruined that poor girl Jenny so now she's obsessively stalking you or something and she's scaring the hell out of me. So I think the best thing to do is just leave me alone so I can wait out my time here until I can get back to my real life. You know, without getting murdered in my sleep."

"Um," he says again, and then, "Oh God, don't cry."

"I'm not crying!" I'm a mess and my eyes are tearing up and my nose feels like it's swelling. I glance around at the back of the buildings that are all in this strange semicircle around the big grass lawn. We're behind them, facing a bunch of trees. I think it's a forest and I know if I go in there, there is a particularly good chance that I will never find my way out again.

"Come here," Eric says, putting his arms out to hug me.

"Forget it," I say, sniffling. I make at least one really gross noise. Not fabulous.

"What? Why?"

"You'll probably feel me up."

He laughs, and chokes out, "Probably." And then I laugh too, laughing and crying. I must be PMSing. He puts his arms out again, and this time I step into them and it's weird. . . . This is what Jennifer must have meant — he's a total player, but right now I don't care, because he's got one hand in the back of my hair, kinda massaging the nape of my neck, and the other hand is rubbing up and down my spine.

"I need a tissue," I say. I wipe my nose and eyes on the back of my hand before resting my forehead against his shoulder.

"God, I hope you didn't just wipe that on my shoulder."

"No, on my hand."

"Really? That's so sexy. Are you trying to turn me on?"

"Yeah." I laugh again. "I hate that I'm so transparent."

He pulls away, his hands on my shoulders, and looks me in the face. "Ready to go back in there?"

"Not so much. Can we go for a walk?"

He hedges. "I dunno. You're likely to miss something and then get a demerit and then —"

"I don't care. What's the worst thing that could happen?"

"They'll send you home and you'll lose your entire tuition."

"Boo hiss," I say, turning toward the woods. Eric follows me. "So what is it that you do here? Just hang out?"

"Yeah, when I'm on break. My mother is the program head."

"We met."

He smiles. "She's a bit much sometimes."

"Oh, I know. We met," I repeat. In a clearing a ways away, a large tree has fallen over. I head toward it. Eric walks beside me, with his hands in his low, deep pockets.

"What do you do the rest of the time?"

"School, work out, seduce unsuspecting girls in my mother's charge."

I shoot him a look and he holds his hands up in front of him. "Kidding, geez."

"That's not what I hear."

"Oh yeah, from who?" he asks. We reach the clearing, the sun is shining, and there is a slight breeze. It's perfect. Nature isn't so bad after all, I suppose. I sit down on the tree, which has bark that digs into my butt a little. Eric sits down on the grass next to my feet. He's not as close as he was the last time, but he's still sitting close. I think of the last boy I sat next to and wonder what D is doing.

I give him a look and he nods. "Jennifer," he guesses.

"Jennifer told me to stay away from you. That you were a player and that you would probably seduce me if you had half the chance." I don't add that I thought Jennifer was a total wack job, or that I thought she was right. Or that I wasn't sure I wouldn't like it.

Instead of doing what I thought he'd do, sigh and dispute the whole thing, he just stays quiet for a moment and then says, "Jenny's my ex."

"No kidding," I snort.

"She dumped me a couple of months ago, and we seemed to be OK with it, until she saw me out with this other girl from town. Then she lost it and now I don't know."

"She dumped you?" I ask. Sometimes girls are so insane.

"Yeah, I mean, I know — it's really hard to comprehend. I'm such a specimen," he says, lying back on the ground. He folds his arms behind his head, making his chest seem wide.

I cough politely. "Are you still seeing this other girl?"

"No," he says. I am pleased. I have no idea why, but I am pleased.

"That's too bad."

"Is it?" he asks, sitting up. Suddenly he seems very close. What is going on here?

"Look," I say, scooting back a few inches. "I don't know what's going on. The girls in there are crazy. Your ex-girlfriend is telling me that you're likely to seduce anything with two legs, and from how you're acting, it's like she's right."

"Isn't it just as easy to imagine that I just like you?"

"You like me?" I ask. He nods. "You like me? You don't know me."

"Well — that's disputable," he says, lying back down again.

89

"It's not disputable. We met yesterday. You don't know anything about me, other than the fact that my nose runs when I cry and that I don't like nature!"

"Actually . . ." he says, and suddenly he looks kind of uncomfortable.

"Spit it out," I say, tensing, waiting for the worst. I'm not sure what the worst is, but somehow I feel like I'm about to get it. He leans back onto the grass and stretches out. He crosses his ankles and folds his arms over his eyes to block out the sun. "I might know you a little more than you think."

"How so?"

"I read your application material."

"Come again?"

"I read your application material."

"Yes," I say, kneeling next to him, and kneel-crawling closer to his face, so I can pull his hands away from his eyes to find out if he's serious or not. "I got that the first time. But what you do mean you read my application material?"

"Well, I was helping my mom out in the office when your material came in, and I sort of glanced at it."

"They just let anyone look at that stuff? What happened to privacy?" I stand up and begin pacing. He sits up and looks at me.

"It's private."

"How private can it be . . . oh." I pause, noticing the blush creeping up his neck. "You weren't supposed to see it."

"Right."

"And you looked anyway."

"Right."

"And the picture?"

He turns bright red then. I sigh and sit down. Jeez. This is weird. I mean, it's not weird that some guy likes me, because who could blame him, really? But I don't think I've ever been on the boy side of the girly stalking experience. It's kinda flattering, in a creepy way.

"When did my application come in?"

"About four months ago."

"Let me get this straight. You saw something you weren't supposed to see," (he nods) "then you read something you weren't supposed to read," (nods again) "and then you copied the picture from my application?" (One final, slightly delayed nod)

"Oh my God. You still have it in your pocket, don't you?" I ask.

"Maybe."

I open my mouth to say something. Then close it. Then open it — seriously. What does one say to this? *You're a freak? Thank you? Get away from me? Let's make out? I like your nail polish?*

"Look, just because you read that doesn't mean you really know anything about me."

"I get that."

"So . . ."

"So, I MySpaced you."

"You what?"

"I looked you up on MySpace."

I sat down again. "You MyStalked me."

"Yes."

"And you think this is normal?"

"No, not really."

"Pfft," I scoff. "I mean, should I believe that?"

"Well, it is a strange little introduction. . . ."

"A little?"

"But when I read that material you sent, you were just so funny . . . and then, I don't know, it's not like you were my type either."

My eyebrows rise at this. I'm not *his* type? He's stalking me and I'm not his type?

"I mean, I didn't go around looking for people who are like you, but something about what you wrote on your application just caught my attention and made me laugh and I wanted to know more about you. So . . . so, I MySpaced you."

My mind began reeling through all the things that were on my MySpace page. Holy crap. Everything. My entire life is on my MySpace page.

"I just liked you. The more I read, the more I liked. I had to con my way into getting to be the one who picked you up."

I looked at him and he had this weird earnest look on his fact that I didn't know what to do with. I thought about it for a second and wondered, Could I like him? Could I like this guy? I mean, he's not my type but he's funny and witty and obviously good around the Internet and not above a little obstruction of the privacy regulations. That said, he doesn't have any sense of personal boundaries (at all) and . . . and . . . he's not D.

It takes me a moment to let that sink in. It doesn't matter that Eric is totally cute and totally here and obviously adorable in an alternative punk sort of way. And it doesn't matter that he's a great flirt or that he looks like he'd be an amazing kisser. But what about D? How could I trust my own judgment when it comes to who is good for me and who isn't?

"Eric, I don't know what to say — I'm really flattered."

"Uh-oh," he says, sitting up.

"But I'm sorta seeing someone else." I'm a liar. And a bad person. And a liar.

"You are?"

"Yes," I snap. "I am. Why is that so hard to believe?"

"Well, your MySpace page says you're single. And . . . I dunno, I guess I just didn't think that I'd meet someone like you and you'd be dating someone."

I blush a little. "Well, I'm not dating. Not really."

"Oh?"

"It's someone I've liked for a long time. And . . . well, I don't know. This is all very confusing. It's just bad timing.

I mean . . . I don't even know if I even like him. I thought I did but then I kissed him and it felt all wrong, but we haven't really even talked about it and then I lied to him and . . ."

He stands up, brushing his hands on his pants. "No, no. Kimono, right?" (I nod.) "You don't need to explain anything." He smiles in his quirky crooked way, and for half a second I want to take it all back and just grab and kiss him. OK, weird. "Look, I knew from the moment I read your application that I had to try. But I knew there was a chance, a good chance, that you were probably taken or might be uninterested."

"Uninterested?" I ask, smiling.

"Yeah, I mean, there was always a chance that you had some sort of head injury. I didn't look at your medical records. I'm not totally without morals."

"Well, morally — isn't it bad that you looked at *any* of it?" I say, thinking of the fact that he saw my weight. UGH.

"No, that's ethically bad behavior. Morally, I'm fine."

"Oh, good."

"Yeah."

"Maybe we should get back now," I say, turning back toward the buildings.

"You're going to have to tell me about this guy," he says, walking back with me — standing a few inches farther away than he did on the walk over. "I mean, I'm going to have to undercut him any chance I get. So you might as well give me some fodder. Is he way too old for you? Does he get bad grades?

Is he your second cousin? Does he talk with his mouth full? Really, anything you can do to help . . ."

I laugh. "I'll be sure to compile a complete dossier."

"Perfect." We reach the building and he holds the door open for me. "Friends, then?"

"Sure, why not." I smile.

"You know we can't really be friends," he says, leaning over to whisper in my ear.

"No?"

"Of course not. I'm obviously madly in love with you and you're obviously madly in love with me but better at hiding it."

"Again, I'm so transparent."

He smiles and pulls the door wider so I can walk by. At the last minute I stop and he looks hopeful for half a second before glancing down to see my hand extended. "Picture, please."

"But what will I do during candlelit baths?" he says, making an extremely cute "innocent face" that I don't buy for even a moment.

"Picture," I say more urgently, and he shrugs, pulling a folded piece of paper out of his back pocket and putting it in my hand.

I'm in the building, the door shutting behind me again when I hear something that sounds a lot like "have another copy at home."

Riley Swain
New Horizons
19 School House Road
Bangor, NY 19119

Dear Ms. Swain,

I'd like to thank you for the very complimentary letter that you sent earlier this week. We rarely receive such high commendations from the general public and it's nice to know that you feel that the "CIA is a highly underrated public watchdog" and that you would "give us all a raise." From your lips to the director's ears.

To answer your questions:

1) If certain substances were present at the time, it *is* possible to identify whether or not a piece of paper was involved in bath-related activities. Unfortunately we feel that it is a waste of taxpayers' money to identify and implement the type of forensic studies necessary — so I will be unable to assist you further in this regard.

2) It is not illegal, or against national public security, to be "fugly" although I sometimes agree that it should be.

3) We do not know if Elvis is still alive. If we did, we would not tell you.

4) I do not drink, not even wine.

Sincerely,
Adam Priest
Director of Public Safety and Security
Central Intelligence Agency

Encl: Picture of R.S.

ATTACK OF THE THIN PEOPLE

I turn and let the door shut behind me in the main dormitory. I figure I'll head up to my room and grab my schedule to see where the heck I'm supposed to be. Is there a spa day? Maybe some light Pilates? Yoga? Do we talk about our feelings in big groups and whine about chocolate?

"Ms. Swain, what are you doing here?" Mrs. Hotra asks.

I look down at my legs. It should be obvious what I'm doing here.

"Walking?"

"That's apparent, Ms. Swain. What isn't as apparent is why you haven't reported to your behavioral coach for your orientation session."

"My behavioral coach?"

"Ms. Swain," Mrs. Hotra says, with a deep sigh. Ugh, it's like my father revisited. I wonder if she has a BlackBerry. "I think that your lackadaisical attitude is going to hinder your progress here at New Horizons and I want to make it clear, from the very beginning, that this isn't appropriate behavior.

Not for you, not for anyone. We expect every participant to be self-monitoring and motivating. Not only to one's self, but to one another. Am I making myself clear?"

No, not at all. But it sure did sound like great brochure copy.

"Not really."

"I expect that you'll become more familiar with our expectations of our program in detention this evening," she responds.

Detention? Detention on spring break?

"Perhaps that will help you to remember to familiarize yourself with the materials, schedules, and menus that we provided you with, before another problem occurs."

I spot Jennifer down the hall, hiding behind an open door. Her pointy little shoes are sticking out. Witch.

"Materials?"

"Yes, Ms. Swain, the materials that Jennifer gave you yesterday evening?"

Ah. I see.

I turn to Mrs. Hotra. "I understand completely. I think it's great that New Horizons participants take responsibility for their actions, and the ones who don't should be reprimanded."

I felt, if not saw, Jennifer twitch behind her door.

"Exactly, Ms. Swain, I'm glad you understand," she says, pulling down the front of her pink suit-style jacket before brushing an invisible piece of lint off her shoulder. "I expect you to report to your BC right away, and I'll see you this evening in detention."

Mrs. Hotra walks away, her chunky-heeled shoes clumping on the ceramic tiles. When she's out of hearing range I turn toward Jennifer.

"I sure wish I had received those materials, Jennifer," I say loudly. She steps out from behind the door after a moment's hesitation, probably trying to decide if she could run and hide.

"I'm sure Eric can catch you up on how we do things here at New," she says before walking away, leaving me with my jaw on the floor. I can't believe this chick.

My GC is exactly how I pictured her.

Her name is Katie Wilhelm. Petite. Smiles a lot. Wears little glasses, like she went to an Ivy League school.

"Where did you go to college?" I ask.

She shifts in her chair. "I graduated from Emerson and then went to Yale for my PhD in psych."

Yup.

"Wow, you have a PhD from Yale and now you work in upstate New York as a GC?"

"BC."

"Hmm?"

"Behavioral Coach. BC."

"Oh, right, a BC. So you spent — what, like, fifty thousand dollars and seven years to work here?"

"Nine."

"Nine what?"

"Nine years," she says calmly.

"Nine years is a long time."

"True," she says, "but it goes quickly when you're doing what you enjoy."

I feel a lesson coming on, so I cut it off before she has a chance to tell me the virtues of living in the moment or becoming one with my world, whatever.

"So what do we do here?" I ask, glancing around the office. On the walls there are pictures of her with a bunch of different "program participants." I wonder if she just likes taking pictures with fat girls. That fat girls really make her look thinner than she already is, and I wonder if she keeps those pictures around to remind herself that she isn't really one of us. That even though she is working here, she isn't really a part of our problems.

"Well," she says, "every day — outside of weekends —"

"Of course." I nod.

"We'll meet to talk about your progress and motivation. We'll talk about making decisions and stress and how it affects all that you do. We'll review the material in your journal and your responses to assignments that I ask you to do. But mostly, we'll just talk."

"Just talk?" I ask. I focus on a small picture of Ms. Wilhelm hugging a girl — probably a student. She's exactly the same height as Ms. Wilhelm but twice as wide. It looks grotesquely like a "before" and "after" picture — but with the images embracing each other. It makes me feel uncomfortable.

"Yup," she says, "talk about whatever you want to talk about. However you're feeling. Sometimes I'll ask questions, but basically — I want you to just talk to me."

"I have a question." She beams, like seriously. "Does therapy actually ever work? Because it seems like once a person starts going — and I know a lot of people who go — that they never stop."

"Well, it doesn't work for everyone, but it does work."

"So, if I come here and talk to you, my problems will go away?" I ask, thinking of Jennifer suddenly disappearing and Eric appearing in her spot.

"It doesn't work like that, Riley," she says, smiling (still).

"How *does* it work?"

"Well, we talk and hopefully you come away learning something about yourself, maybe seeing things from a new perspective. And then maybe being able to change things if you can."

"Seriously?" I ask. "That's it?"

"That's it. It's not magic, Riley. It's a lot of hard work. But we'll do it together."

"Well, that's fine, but what you're basically saying is that we talk. Or rather, I talk." (She nods.) "And then I am supposedly going to see something from a new perspective" (she nods again) "and then I have to change?" (Nodding, enthusiastically now)

"Wow," I continue, looking at her — she looks like she feels she's had a breakthrough moment. I hate to rain on her parade. "What a crock."

"Why do you think that's a crock, Riley?"

"Well, I talk to people all the time. I analyze things all the time. I change my opinion about things all the time, but I don't feel like I've made any momentous leaps. You're saying the thing that I've been missing is a therapist to listen to me?"

"Not only listen but to ask guiding questions."

"I don't know. Sounds sketchy," I say, shifting in the chair I'm sitting in. I was offered the couch when I came in — but thought it looked kind of ratty. Like a million fat girls cried on that couch. No, thank you.

She just laughs.

"So, you basically spent, like, fifty K so you could listen to me talk."

"Something like that," she says.

"Why?"

"Because I want to help."

"That's sweet," I say, fiddling with my fingers and avoiding eye contact. I want to call bullshit. Help who? Help what? You want to help, get me out of detention for this evening — now there is a way you can help.

"Have you ever been fat?" I ask.

She shakes her head. "Nooooo . . ." (she draws this out like her answer might change midword) "but I took special training and certification in dealing with the behavior modification of adolescents with body and self-esteem issues."

"So, you took a class on thinking like a fat chick."

"Something like that."

"Weird."

"Why is that weird?"

I look up from the spot on the carpet that I had been focusing on without even realizing it and glance at her before putting my eyes back down again. "It's like nuns giving marital and sex advice."

"And you think they can't?"

"I don't think a skinny girl can understand what it means to be a fat girl because she took a class in it."

"That's understandable."

"Maybe you should eat more, get fat, and then you can really understand." She shifts in her seat. "I mean, if you're really interested in helping, it kind of makes sense."

"Hmm. It's something to think about," she prevaricates. "For both of us."

"I think it sounds great. Let me know if you need any help."

"OK," she says.

"OK?"

"OK, our time's up."

103

I begin to laugh. Typical. I wonder if there is a timer or if it just becomes too painful for her to listen to and then magically, time is up.

"It's nice meeting you, Riley. I'll see you tomorrow for fifteen minutes before morning announcements, and make sure you come in on time, so those with appointments after you aren't displaced."

Yeah. Right. I nod.

"Riley," she says as I am walking out the door. "I don't have to be overweight to know what it means to be unhappy with my body."

"Right," I say, and add because I think she might want to know, "I don't have to be depressed and a head case just because I'm overweight. I don't belong here."

"Right," she responds. "See you tomorrow."

"Right." I close the door after me as she bends her head over her desk and jots notes about how I'm opening up nicely and am mentally inquisitive but entirely too stuck on the issue of my weight. But I know she isn't writing anything about it being a mistake that I'm here.

I wonder if I can trick her into becoming fat. Has anyone ever been peer-pressured into overeating? I'm going to go see if I can order Twinkies online so I can plant them around her office.

CRUEL AND UNUSUAL PUNISHMENT

By Monday afternoon I'm ready to call the police and claim cruel and unusual punishment. First they made me do a feel-good session with my BC and then after lunch (they called it Thai food, but it was *not* Thai . . . that's like buying a purse at Wal-Mart and calling it Prada) there was a seminar on cooking healthy, and finally afternoon exercise.

"Come on, ladies, I want to see you skip!"

Sergeant Bullwhip puts the whistle (I kid you not) that is hanging from a blue cord around her neck into her mouth and gives short bursts. I assume we are supposed to skip like crack addicts to her whistled rhythm.

I wonder how a person becomes a gym teacher (pardon, physical education teacher). Watching Sergeant BW, I think, is it the shorts? Gym teacher shorts must hold allure for some. I wonder if Jennifer likes gym shorts. Stylish.

"Ms. Swain, will you be joining us?" Sergeant calls from across the gym floor. Half the group stops to turn and watch me, wondering if I'm going to start skipping like an idiot.

"I'm not properly equipped for skipping," I call back. Gazes whip from my general direction back to Sarge.

"I don't believe any special equipment is necessary to skip, Ms. Swain." Some of the students buzz at the joke. Whatever.

"I have very large breasts."

That stops the buzz.

"And," I continue, "I don't feel it is physically beneficial for me to skip without the proper . . . support."

Sarge glows a little red in the cheeks. I hope I didn't bring up something inappropriate for gym class. She walks up to me, her whistle dangling between her fingers. Why do I feel like I'm about to earn myself another demerit?

"Ms. Swain, did you know that you were having gym class today?"

"Sort of," I say. "My schedule said physical education."

"And do they have physical education at your high school?" she asks.

"Yes." (The heads are bobbing back and forth faster than the crowds at Wimbledon.)

"And at your high school, are you expected to show up to each and every class prepared or risk failing?" (And the serve, it's over the net. . . .)

"Sort of."

106

"Sort of?"

"Well, every class except for gym," I say. "My old gym teacher knew what having large breasts felt like. She *empathized.*" I finish off with a pointed look at the place on her chest where her boobs should be. VOLLEY!

Her eyes widen and her jaw drops. Nice.

"Skip," she says.

"Huh?"

"Skip NOW," she repeats, louder this time.

I'd like to point out that I start skipping. Not because she scares me, but because I am worried for her. She has turned bright red and there is this HUGE vein sticking out the side of her neck and I am worried that if I don't fix this right away she will have a brain aneurysm and there are probably three or four mini bullwhips at home waiting for Momma Bullwhip to come home and spot them in their weight-lifting exercises. And if Momma Bullwhip doesn't come home, someone will drop a big weight on their neck and die. I can't handle that type of responsibility.

So I skip.

Twenty-five minutes later, she blows her whistle again. Thirty minutes at an accelerated heart rate cannot be good for a girl. All I want is my Pilates mat! My thighs are burning and I'm bent over at the waist.

"You did good, Riley." Sergeant comes over and pats me on the back. I almost smile but she turns around too quickly and I realize that I almost succumbed to the pressures of the place. No wonder all these girls seem happy here. It's like army boot camp. First they break you down physically and then by the time you are sweating and heaving, bent at the waist, they try and pump you up emotionally. Positive and negative reinforcement, and by then you are so into it that you gladly accept any modicum of acceptance they give you.

Hells no.

Plus, I did *well*. Not *good*. Apparently a high school education is not a requirement to be an instructor at New Horizons.

I crawl my way back through to the locker rooms, where there are a bunch of girls already getting naked, without the self-consciousness that they have back home. Where you feel like if you're beautiful you have to get naked early and often, and if you aren't — well, you delay and hide. There is almost an art form to getting naked and changed without showing any bit of skin the entire time. I've got it down to an exact science. . . . I can change my pants without showing thigh or lower midsection, in fourteen seconds flat. Unfortunately I have a harder time doing the shirt thing, but it's fine because I have great breasts (as previously mentioned). Yes, I mention it a lot . . . but as my gram always used to say, "If you got 'em, flaunt them." If you don't got 'em, pad them and then flaunt them.

Where was I? Oh yeah, so all these girls are getting naked without any self-consciousness and I am about five seconds from feeling as if maybe this place isn't so bad. Maybe like attracts like and then like treats like fairly and compassionately because like knows how like hurts.

And then I hear Jennifer say something about Samantha and point in her direction, and Tilly laughing. So goes the like-like theory. And so goes any respect or sympathy I had for Jenny.

But before I go overboard, I watch.

After a few more pointed looks and an overly loud giggle (the kind that only happens when one person wants someone else to know that they are being made fun of), Jenny strolls over to Sam, with Tilly in her wake.

"Hi, Samantha," she says.

"Oh, um, hi, Jenny. Tilly."

I feel like I should cover my eyes. Either Samantha is really oblivious or perhaps nature has gone to her head, because she doesn't see the sharp look in Jenny's eyes and doesn't seem to see the snark coming.

Me? I can see snark coming (and block it) miles in advance, but Sam just sits there smiling, a little confused, like these girls are her friends. I move a little closer, hoping to heck that she is smarter than she looks and knows what to say to deflect.

"Tilly and I were just talking about the picture of the guy you have on your desk," Jenny says, smiling over her shoulder at Tilly before catching my eye. I try to give her a "stop it now and walk away, and you'll remain unharmed" look, but she just scrunches up her nose at me and turns back to Samantha.

"Oh yeah?" Samantha says, pulling her socks on.

"Yeah," Jenny says, her back against the lockers. "I was asking Tilly who it was. I mean, I didn't think it could be your boyfriend. Or is it? I mean, he's really hot."

Samantha starts looking uncomfortable. "He's not my boyfriend."

"I didn't think so, but who *is* he?" Jenny says.

Ugh. I'm going to cut in here. I'm going to regret it, especially since Samantha didn't stick up for me earlier, but it's like watching a goldfish swimming in the shark tank.

"Hey, Sam," I say. "Maybe you could set up Jenny. I mean, she sounds pretty desperate for a new boyfriend."

Two gasps and a head swivel. A little sharper of a turn and I think Tilly's head might've screwed right off. Sweet.

"Riley . . ." Samantha says, but I just look at Jenny and Tilly. Jenny stares me down for a couple of seconds and then tsks her tongue.

"We were only making conversation."

"Me too." I smile. Bitches.

"You know, you are who you hang out with, Samantha," Jenny says, grabbing a bag off the bench before walking away, Tilly in her wake. There is a long pause while we wait for them to make it outside the locker room and before our aisle clears up. I'm waiting around . . . for what? For a thank-you? Somehow I don't think it's going to happen.

"I didn't need you to jump in."

You cannot be serious.

"I was just trying to help," I tell Samantha, stuffing my crap in my bag. Seriously, you try to help someone and it's not like I expected a thank-you — although that would've been nice — but I certainly didn't expect a lecture.

"No, I understand what you were trying to do — but you're leaving here in a couple of weeks and I'll be here for another two years."

Eh. I didn't think of that. And suddenly I wonder if I just made things worse, because Jenny wouldn't turn around and say anything to me. A shark knows better than to go after another shark. Sharks prey on the fish without the big teeth. People like Samantha, who probably don't deserve it except through virtue of not being a shark.

"Look, I'm sorry. I didn't . . . I'm just sorry."

"Forget it," she says, smiling. "It was a good line, though."

"Yeah, it kinda was."

She laughs and for a second I am reminded why I liked her so much that morning.

"So, you have a picture of a hot guy in our room? And I didn't see it? I thought I had radar for that sort of thing."

"I have a picture of my stepbrother, not a hot guy."

"Stepbrother? Honey, if there is no blood in common, there is nothing to —"

"Ew," she says, "you have *got* to stop."

"Fine, fine. Let's get out of here. I have a free period for the next —" I look down at my cell — "forty-three minutes. They do keep you buzzing around here."

"Yeah and if you're late more than three times for any activity, it's a quarter demerit."

I stop in my tracks and turn to face her. "What exactly is the deal with these demerits?"

"Three demerits and you get sent home until the start of the next program."

"And this is bad?"

"I dunno, I guess," she says, walking around me and out of the locker room.

CAN YOU FALL
FOR SOMEONE
OVER VOICE MAIL?

I walk with Samantha back to the Victoria Dorm because she wants to check her e-mail. Once in our room, I make my bed, which only takes thirteen tries and Samantha to show me how. The rest of the room is pretty bare on my side, but it is obvious that Samantha lives here year-round. Her wall is covered with posters, snapshots, letters from friends, quotes, and one big movie poster of *Batman*. I'm not sure which one.

While Sam checks her e-mail (and after I get a quick look at the pic of the boy on Sam's desk — yes, he is hot), I lie on my bed and check my voice messages. Which are as follows:

D: *Hey, Rye — What's up in upstate NY? You haven't called so I'm just checking in. M says you're going to be going on the trip. What changed? But I'm glad you're going to be there. I think we need to talk about what happened. I'm feeling kind of weird about it.*

Dad: *Hello, Riley, it's your father speaking. I hope you're having a fun and productive trip. If it can only be one, I hope it's productive (chortle). I'm calling because Emily left a message saying that there has been a large charge on your credit card recently and wanted to know if your cc has been stolen. Please call Emily back and confirm that you didn't leave your wallet in a cab.*

Marley: *Hey, sweetheart! I'm just hanging out with D and we wanted to say hi and see how you are enjoying your spa vacay! We called the spa first but they said you hadn't checked in yet. I hope everything is good. Call us!*

D: *Hey — you're not mad at me, are you? Call me.*

Dad: *Riley, Emily said the charge was for over three grand for a spa in upstate NY. Call me back right away.*

D: *Did you lose your phone again?*

Eric: *Um, hello, Riley's cell phone. This is Eric's cell phone calling. Eric would like to know if Riley is available to meet tonight after dinner. Perhaps go for a walk so he can further pursue his totally platonic and on-the-level stalking. Please call or text Eric's cell phone back. You have the digits.*

D: *Greetings to the taxi driver who has found this phone. Congratulations! You are now the owner of a three-month-old iPhone. These phones retail for around four hundred dollars but you got it for free because the owner, Riley Swain, can't hold on to a phone to save her life. If you see Riley, tell her to get her ass on the phone — I'm going to start feeling unloved.*

Eric: *So, you haven't called yet. Am I being too forward? Because I've been told that I can be too forward at times, but I know chicks like guys who are openly aggressive. It all goes back to that primitive "me man, you woman" thing, right?*

Delete All Messages?
Yes.

I look through my missed-calls registry and scroll past D's name to click on Eric, who has kindly put his name, number, and a charming picture of himself smiling smugly into the phone for me to find. Except instead of it saying "Eric," it says "Mr. Right."

I laugh loudly so that Samantha turns around and raises her eyebrows. I think of calling D first but just shake my head and hit SEND.

"I knew you couldn't resist me," he says when he picks up.

115

"Wow, Eric," I say, flipping onto my stomach, "I've never been stalked quite like that before."

"Only the best for my girl."

"Eric, I'm not your girl."

"Semantics."

I am still smiling like an idiot, and by now Samantha is watching me carefully and I just shoo her away and turn to face the wall so I won't have to watch her making kissy faces at me.

"So . . ." he says. "Meet me after dinner?"

"I guess. I mean, that's probably the only way I'm going to get you off my back, right?"

"Probably. I can't promise, of course, but really, what other choice do you have?"

"Right," I say, smiling into the phone. "When and where?"

He names a place and a time after dinner but well before lights-out, which I repeat back to him. I'll need to get Sam's help figuring out where this place is, but that's fine. It sounds like she is already listening anyway. I figure I can trust her. I mean, I'm not really trusting her with *anything real* . . . I'm just going to meet him and talk. And tell him again that nothing was going to happen.

I hang up and figure I have to deal with Samantha before I can call D back. Plus, I'd actually want some privacy for *that* conversation.

"OK, nothing is going on," I say, sitting up in bed and turning around.

Her eyebrows are already in the raised position as she drinks from an open can of Diet Pepsi. "Nothing, huh?"

"No, nothing. He called and left some annoying (charming) messages, and I'm going to meet him later to tell him to cut it out."

"I could see the glare from your smile all the way over here."

"Whatever."

"You like him," Samantha sings.

"No, I don't! I like this guy from home."

"Uh-huh."

"Whatever."

"You keep up that great rebuttal and I'll totally start believing you."

I jump off the bed and begin rummaging through my suitcases.

"What are you doing?" Samantha says, glancing over her keyboard at me.

"Looking for something to wear to dinner."

I don't even stop when I hear her laughing. I like to dress for dinner. It has nothing to do with Eric whatsoever. I pick something low-cut and run for the bathroom with my makeup bag.

THEBIGUN17: So now there is a new guy?

RILEDUP: I don't know. I'm not sure I'm over the old guy.

THEBIGUN17: What's the new one like?

RILEDUP: He's a bit of a freak. In that overly assertive I LIKE YOU kind of way.

THEBIGUN17: That's nice, right? A guy who isn't scared to express his feelings?

RILEDUP: Um, it's scary. But kinda nice. I mean, I don't know. I can't tell.

THEBIGUN17: Sure, whatever. Just give him a chance.

RILEDUP: You're not even a little jealous?

THEBIGUN17: What do I have to be jealous over?

RILEDUP: Tell me the truth — you want me to be your girlfriend. You want me to stand this guy up and spend all night on IM with you. Right?

THEBIGUN17: You can't hear me, but I'm laughing really hard.

RILEDUP: Ew.

ROMANCE IS
SO MY THING

Dinner passes uneventfully. Meaning without drama (since Jenny and Tilly sat with a group of girls on the other side of the cafeteria and I sat with Sam and Allie) and without taste (since they served grilled chicken breast, overly steamed broccoli, and iced tea without sweetener).

I must've done something wrong that I'm being punished this way. This is not fair. Prisoners probably eat better than this.

I do spend at least the majority of dinner talking about the really great food that I've eaten in NY, over which Allie seems to salivate and Samantha just rolls her eyes and calls us masochists. Dreamers, not masochists, I retort. Good food is a privilege of a free and open society. To keep us away from it is akin to slavery.

Samantha just rolls her eyes again, but Allie is into it.

After I finish eating, I excuse myself, to which Samantha gives me a highly stylized and overdramatic wink. Ugh. The girl does *not* know how to keep a secret. Instead I brush off my suede skirt (A-line, dramatic yet flattering), dump my tray, and decide it is time to make my way to the meeting place.

Our meeting place is a boathouse by the lake under this really big tree. I get there about fifteen minutes early. Eric is already there.

"You're early," I say.

He stands up from the dock and smiles at me. "You are too. Couldn't stay away?"

"Who, me or you?"

He just smiles and sits down again, patting the dock next to him. Ugh, I am wearing a skirt and not at all in a position to go dock-sitting, but I kick off my sandals and sit down next to him anyway. Then I dip my toes in the water.

"We're early," he says, turning his head toward me.

"Early for what?"

"Well, at dusk, it gets a lot colder and the water is warm, so it gets a little foggy on the water."

"Oh. Fog," I say.

"It's romantic."

"If you say so."

I'm looking out over the water and see small bubbles pop up, then look over at him. "Probably just fish or a turtle or something."

I pull my feet out of the water and slip my sandals back on.

"They won't bite you, Riley," he says, smiling at my toes.

"Can you prove that?"

He shakes his head, but then asks, "So what did you want to talk about?"

"Me?" I start. "You were the one who invited me here. And I just couldn't think of a good enough excuse to stay home."

"Dead aunt."

"Hmm?"

"Kill an aunt. It's always the best excuse for anything that doesn't have an excuse."

"You kill your aunt? First, I try not to murder people, and second, I don't have any aunts. I do have a soon-to-be stepmother I could sacrifice willingly."

"No, I mean, if you need a good excuse, you say your aunt died. People can't really question that without sounding like a complete jerk," he says, reaching down into the water and pulling out a weed. Gross. "Plus, then you can go back to normal the next day because nobody will think badly about you for not overly mourning an aunt. Grandparents get tricky."

"Wow," I say, staring. "You're a sociopath."

"Not really. It's all hypothetical."

"Well, as someone who has lost a parent, at least I could pull it off," I say, smiling at him. But he's not smiling back.

"Sorry. Wow. That was really insensitive of me," he says softly.

"No, I mean, not really. I mean, it's fine, I was kidding. . . . I guess I was being insensitive," I say, then I take a deep breath. "I don't normally talk about . . ."

"Yeah, I mean, you don't have to talk about it now," he says, turning to face me. "I mean, you can if you want to, but if you'd rather not, it's cool."

"There's not much to talk about, really. I don't remember that much of it."

"How old were you?" he asks.

"Four," I say.

"That's really young," he says. "I don't know. My mom's a pain in the ass, but I don't know what I would've done without her. Especially after Dad left. She was great. She moved us here and managed everything. I just, I don't know, you're really strong."

"No I'm not," I say, and I wonder about his mom and his relationship with her. He seems to like her a lot. I wonder whether I would like *my* mom. I need to change the subject.

"You OK, Riley?"

"Yeah," I say. "What's the story with Jenny?"

He looks startled for a minute, but if he thinks I'm crazy he doesn't say anything. Instead he crosses his arms in front of him over his knees and groans.

"Did you love her?"

"Yes."

Death knell. He's not supposed to say yes . . . at the very least, he wasn't supposed to say it so fast and so real.

"Why?" I ask, mainly because I'm a masochist at some level and I want to know what she has that I don't. I want to see where I am lacking. I mean, maybe I can be more amazing than I already am. Maybe I can fix this.

"We've always been . . . I just know her. She knows me," he says. He's got this winsome smile on his face (vomit) and I want to make him hurt so I can see that smile go away, but I bite my lip. I bite it so hard that I actually tear up. I turn away so he doesn't see the tear and think it's him and these words of love.

"Well," I say. "I'm not sure if that's amazingly beautiful or the most tragic thing I've ever heard."

"Thanks." He sighs. The moment is over. The winsome smile is gone. I didn't tear it from his face but I definitely removed it. She put the smile there. I take it away. This is not how I want it to be.

"And now that you're not seeing her? Do you miss her?" I ask, preparing myself for the answer.

"No, I don't miss her."

I let out a breath I didn't even know I was holding and look over at him. He puts his hand out, entwines the tips of his fingers between mine, pulling my hand closer. Then loosens them and entwines them more, tighter.

We sit there, not talking, staring at the water . . . and slowly as it begins to get darker, and the temperature drops, I wish I wasn't wearing a sleeveless shirt. A slow mist starts to rise off the water. When the moon comes out, it's almost iridescent, and beautiful.

"This nature stuff is pretty," I tell him. I expect him to say something kitschy, but he just nods and keeps looking out at the water. There are croaking sounds in the background, and I feel like I'm on a movie set for the perfect outdoor date. I turn and look at him. He's looking at me. I smile and he smiles back.

I'm not thinking straight, I know I'm not, because I'm thinking about how great it would be if he kissed me right now.

I'm thinking about whether or not my palm is sweaty. His isn't and I like that about him. I'm thinking that my fingers are fat and I hate that. I'm thinking that I want him to kiss me and wondering why he hasn't and if it would be rude of me to ask. I'm wondering what will happen if I do ask him, will it make him think that . . . well, I don't know what I think right now. All I know is that I didn't call D back yet, and I'm only feeling a little bit guilty about that.

But I don't know what D has to say to me, and if I'm going to be completely honest with myself, I'm not sure I want to know. I mean, he has been hanging out with Marley a lot, so maybe he's calling just to tell me that he doesn't want anything to do with me, and for the first time in months I don't feel like

124

that would be the worst thing that could happen to me. It won't wreck me.

I'm thinking of a lot of things.

"If you were interested, you would've kissed me by now, right?" I ask softly. Eric laughs, but doesn't say anything.

"Oh God," I say, falling backward onto the dock — so I'm dangling off at the knee, but otherwise, lying down under the dusky sky. "Did I just sexually assault you?"

"It was more like peer pressure."

Ugh! I pull my hand away and roll over. "This is embarrassing," I say.

"No, no," he says. "Come over here."

"No, I can't," I tell him, still face in dock. Ew. I'm going to get a splinter. I'm still thinking except now half of my thoughts have been hijacked by embarrassment.

"Look, turn around for a second."

I turn around to face him, and he's up on one elbow. He leans over and I tilt my head up, but he puts his face next to mine, so our cheeks are touching and inhales deeply and I'm glad that I put vanilla perfume on. I smell like baked goods, which is never fully bad, and so what if the mosquitoes love me. . . .

"No," he says.

"No?" I repeat. "No what?" I say. His face is still in the crook of my neck, and I can hear him laugh softly against my skin. It sends tingles up and down my arms. Gooseflesh. I've always hated that word.

125

"No, I wouldn't necessarily have kissed you. It's difficult to lie next to someone you're attracted to and not kiss them, but I was trying to control myself. I'm a little nervous."

My legs are buzzing now. My hands feel like they don't belong to me, and this is the most awkward first kiss I've ever had. I feel like I'm not in full control of my body — I don't know where to put my arms, under me, under him, around him? He leans over me a little more, and he strokes my cheek, his palm warm against my face.

Oh. My.

He bends his face down, his lips meet mine, and I can smell his lip balm. I smile at that. And his lips are so soft, and I peek through my lashes and his eyes are closed . . . then his lips move against mine and I stop thinking completely.

SUSCEPTIBLE TO THE WILES OF MEN

THEBIGUN17: So now you're making out with two guys?

RILEDUP: UGH! Don't say it like that.

THEBIGUN17: But that's what it is. Isn't it? You kissed D and decided he wasn't the one, which is really kind of weird. And then you kissed this other guy and . . .

RILEDUP: And . . . I didn't decide anything.

THEBIGUN17: When are you going to tell D where you are?

RILEDUP: Never.

THEBIGUN17: You have to.

RILEDUP: I called him and got his voice mail. I take that as a sign that he's not meant to know.

THEBIGUN17: Well, I vote for the new guy.

RILEDUP: Why's that?

THEBIGUN17: You can't even tell D where you are. What kind of relationship can you have when you can't even have simple honesty?

RILEDUP: Honesty is overrated.

THEBIGUN17: I'm glad you think so.

Back in my room, with Samantha asleep, I think some more. When did this get so confusing? A week ago, screw it — three days ago — I wouldn't have put off answering D's calls, and if I saw I had missed a call of his, I would've been on the phone so fast . . . no wonder he thought I lost my phone again. He has never known a time when I wasn't at his beck and call, ready and willing to talk to him for however long and in whatever venue he wanted.

I start getting a little upset with myself. Am I such a pushover? What happened to female strength of personality? Am I just like Marley and Jenny? Am I subject to all the rules that said a man would define my behavior?

I think of all the times that D wanted to hang out and I would cancel any plans I had to be with him. And then I think of all the times that he canceled on me and I forgave him, didn't even ask for a reason.

I pick up the phone and when his snarky voice tells me I could leave him a message, I leave him one.

"Hey, D — it's Riley. Look, I know this is going to seem like it comes out of left field, but I've been thinking about this a lot lately and — well, I just don't know about our relationship. I've always thought of you as my best friend, but I'm not really sure. I mean, I feel like I'm always there for you and you're there when it's convenient to be. But I'm not sure you'd be there if I really needed you. Then again, maybe I'm not such a great friend to you. I love you, or at least I think I do. You're my best friend, and I want more but I don't think I want more with you, and perhaps I can't be a good friend to you because of that. Maybe because we don't fit this way, everything we have is tainted? I don't know. I just know that I'm upset right now and I wish you were here so we could just talk it out. But I feel like there are things I can't tell you. But I want to. Call me."

Hours later, I bury my head in my pillow and cry about this. I wish I could erase that message and pretend it didn't happen. I even consider texting him that I am sorry and the whole thing is a gag, but in the end I don't. In the end, I simply go wash the makeup off my face and crawl into bed. Instead of calling and apologizing, I tell myself to stay calm. *He's your friend*, I tell myself, *he'll know how to handle this. He'll understand why you lied and he'll forget about the kiss and he'll forgive you.*

I fall asleep wondering what the right thing, in this scenario, is.

When I wake up Tuesday morning, the first thing I think about is Eric. I smile and cuddle farther down under my blankets and snuggle my pillow a little. I feel good, I mean really good, for about two minutes before I remember the voice mail I left D before I conked off to sleep.

I reach for my phone, opening the screen — no new messages. No missed calls. He hasn't even called me.

Okay. I poured my heart out to him and at the very least, I'd expect some sort of response. Something, anything, even if it was just him telling me never to drunk-dial him again. But instead I get nothing and I wonder if that's normal for us, if this is how it's always been and I've just been covering up for him for the past couple of years. Could I have been so blind?

By the time I concede that, yes, I definitely could've been so blind, I'm having these major attacks of self-confidence. What if I don't love D, what if I never really loved D? What have I been doing the past few years? I feel like I am going to cry.

And do I really even like Eric, or is it just so different that it feels real? I feel like I'm not in any position to make any decisions about love, like, friendship. Instead I just lie in bed, staring at the water stain on my ceiling until Sam leans over to see if I'm still awake.

"Need to pee?" she asks. I smile. "What's the matter?"

"I don't think I love him."

"Eric?"

"D."

"D — what?"

"D, my friend D. I thought I was in love with him and now I'm not so sure."

She sighs and sits on the edge of her bed, facing me. "That happens," she says softly, and it makes me wonder who she's thinking of.

"It's just that sometimes I think he's amazing. Like, he

must love me because he spends all his time with me and because he's always telling me how much he adores me and . . . and . . ."

"He sounds like a really great friend," she says.

"Yeah, my best."

"So what's the problem?" Sam asks.

"It's just that I thought I was in love with him. For real. And now . . ."

"Now, with Eric to compare him to, you're not sure," she states, like it's obvious.

"Do you think I'm an idiot?"

"Why would I think that?"

"For falling for a guy I just met, who probably screws every girl who comes through here."

"Actually, I never saw him with anyone other than Jenny. And even that . . . well, it wasn't exactly what I would consider a healthy relationship. He never seemed really happy with her; he always seemed like he was trying to make *her* happy. You know?"

I nod.

"I guess I think of love as being two people who make each other happy, not just one person constantly striving to make sure the other person's needs are met."

"I told him he wasn't my type."

"Eric? What did he say?"

"He said maybe my type isn't right for me."

"Maybe he's correct?"

131

"Maybe," I say, flipping onto my side to face her. "Don't tell him. He's smug enough."

"My lips are sealed," she says. "Breakfast in ten — I'll meet you down there?" I nod, and as she picks up her stuff, my phone buzzes. D?

"Hey, Riley?" I look up at her. "Maybe you should stop looking for reasons to reject Eric. I mean, he might be good for you. Maybe you should let him be good for you?" She pauses a moment inside the door and then leaves, closing the door behind her. I pick up my phone; my blood pulses in double time in my chest.

I flick it on and it's a message from Eric. A picture of the lake appears on my phone, with a note saying, *Thanks for the honest conversation.* I smile at the phone and tuck it under my pillow and snuggle it for another minute before I have to get up and face the day.

Tuesday turns out to be a good day. I mean, good as good can be. There are some weird soy chicken nuggets on my lunch tray — and although they taste nothing like chicken, they have a chicken nugget texture (which, if you think about it, is really gross, so I try not to think about it at all), and I double-dip them in this weird low-sodium, low-sugar (low-taste) BBQ sauce. It's almost like McDonald's . . . OK, not so much. But it is better than the crap they gave us for breakfast, egg whites. Seriously, who eats just egg whites?

Allie and I have our first real, nonfood-related conversation (although at lunch we talk about how great french fries are). She's ridiculously obsessed with the eighties. When I see her today she's wearing a David Bowie T-shirt.

"Who's that?" I ask, pointing at her chest. David Bowie is stretched across some seriously big boobage.

"Are you kidding me?" she responds, her mouth gaping open. Sam and another girl, Kristine, shake their heads and make throat-cutting gestures at me, all wild-eyed. What?

"This is David Bowie."

"Oh, I thought he looked famliar. I mean, as familiar as a blond, Brit-looking guy can look." I smile for about five seconds before she launches into a rant about British music being the catalyst for major worldwide political, artistic, and social changes. This can't have been the first time she's gone on this rant, as the others mime along with her at times, causing me to stifle a giggle and Allie to turn around and stare at them until they stop.

Four hours later I'm whistling a different tune. There is something sadistic about mile-long hikes in the wilderness. First they made me carry my own pack — which was hell. I mean, water bottle, sure, I get hydration, but why do I need all this other crap?

"OK, ladies, we're going to set up here for the night. Unload your packs."

"Excusez-moi?"

Sargeant Bullwhip turns to look at me. "What's the matter, Riley?"

"Did you just say, *for the night?*" I glance around at the other girls. Sam is a few feet away from me, unloading her pack with what looks like a small tent! *Holy crap, they expect us to stay out here. All night?*

"Yes, Riley, for the night. It's called camping because you set up camp. And stay. Outside," she responds, speaking slower and slower as if my brain were mulch and couldn't comprehend simple English. Then again, she is right.

"What you're telling me is that my father is paying good money, a lot of good money, so I can sleep outside?"

"Yes."

"Oh," I say, throwing my bag down on the ground. "That's just great."

It takes me forty-five minutes longer than the slowest girl to pitch my own tent. It's small, simple, has directions (in pictures), and because I am so frustrated, I can't even process simple line drawings.

"Hey, nature girl," Eric says, walking up the hill. "Need some help with that?"

"No," I say, almost breaking one of the support sticks in half. "I hate nature."

"You don't hate nature, you hate nature without me," he says, picking up the directions and flipping them over. "Give me five minutes and I'll have this baby looking like the Ramada."

Twenty-five minutes later, no Ramada.

"The Ramada, huh?" I ask.

"I hate nature," he says, kicking the pile of tent fixings.

"Aw, you don't hate nature, you hate the same thing I hate. Camping equipment," I say, smiling at him — sure that I'm smiling at him the same way he's smiling at me, and it's cool. And my brain suddenly thinks: *I could fall in love with him.*

"Wow?" he asks.

"What?"

"You just said wow."

"I did?"

"Yup. What were you thinkin' about?"

"Nothing!" I say, scrambling away. I can't fall in love with him. I can't — I mean, if I fall in love with him, then I definitely am not in love with D. Can you be in love with two boys at once? Maybe. But if I'm not in love with D and I thought I was ... then maybe I *think* I could love Eric and I really can't. Maybe I can't love anyone! How can you know?

"Samantha!"

Samantha comes running over, hearing the terror in my voice. Eric is staring at me like I'm loony. In fact, a lot of people are staring at me like I'm loony. A girl who had her tent close to mine picks it up and moves it away a few feet farther uphill.

"What's the matter?"

"I can't put my tent up."

Five minutes later, I have the Ramada.

By the time it gets dark, I'm in love with nature again. I never realized how amazing it could be, sitting next to a really big bonfire. We're in this area called Piney Woods, and it is just this clearing a few hundred feet away from a different part of the lake than where the buildings are. But there is this huge space for bonfires, and surrounding the space are these really old, really tall pine trees. The trunks of these trees go up forever, and there are only branches at the very top, and they are so tall that the glow and flickering from the fire barely touches them. And it smells like pine.

"I love it here," I tell Samantha, who is sitting next to me, making low-fat s'mores (seriously, what's the point?).

"Yeah, it's pretty."

"No, I mean, I *love* it here." I look across the fire at Eric, who is reloading the coolers that carried our dinner up the mountain in the back of a minivan, which he must've driven up.

"Uh-huh," she says, not paying attention.

Jenny walks up behind Eric and taps him on the shoulder. She's studiously avoiding my gaze, and I'm staring at her as hard as I can. She asks him something and he replies something.

Samantha is talking to me, but I'm trying my best to learn how to lip-read. I can't breathe as Eric gets up after resetting some logs in the fire and wiping his hands on his pants. He looks over the fire at me, but I look away quickly. I don't want him to think I'm watching (even though I am). Or that I care that he's talking to his ex-girlfriend (even though I do). Or that I know he's getting up to go talk to her in the dark woods, alone (even though I'm about to fall apart).

It gets dark, and the girls are all bundled under sweatshirts and blankets, because it's not quite warm enough to go without, but the air feels cold and clean, scented with pine and sizzling with the sound of gasping wood, burning and breaking in the fire.

If I were a smart girl, I'd get up and cut them off. I'd "accidentally happen upon them in the woods" and ruin their private little tête-à-tête. If I were smart . . . but I'm an idiot.

I'm having another dream. This time it isn't Colin Firth, it's D who is kissing me. He's smiling at me and one moment we're sitting on the dock at the lake, looking over the water — and the next he's trying to help me put up a tent. And then he's kissing me again, but it doesn't feel right and I know — even in my confused sleep-state — I know it's not right.

And then I'm dreaming that I'm in NY, with Eric. That I'm sitting on the stoop of my building, and he's got a cigarette lit, and is ranting up and down the sidewalk, the way D always does. And this doesn't feel right either, so I grab him by the hand and pull him closer to me, and he looks confused by what I'm doing. And I tell him to kiss me. And he shakes his head, but I insist and his lips are on mine. First hesitant, and then insistent . . . and my mind whirls.

Then we're both in the woods and he's calling my name . . . *Riley, Riley . . . Riley . . .*

"Riley . . ."

I blink once. It's still nighttime. I close my eyes. I don't know what woke me up, but I want to figure out what happens next in this dream. If it's going where I think it's going — well, I want to be there for it.

"Riley, wake up," a voice whispers, and something nudges my foot. I wake up, enough to realize that it's definitely still nighttime, but more than that — it's raining.

"What's going on?"

"Come out here," he says. It's Eric. He's outside my tent. Apparently in the middle of the night, in the rain. And I *know* that this is not a good thing. I mean, it's a good thing, but it's not a good thing. I'm going to get in serious trouble if he gets caught. I sit up and my head brushes up against the fabric of the tent, and a film of moisture condenses on the inside. *Eeehh*!

"What's the matter?" he whispers loudly.

"Rain is coming in! I'm going to get wet."

I hear him huff outside. I guess he isn't going to sympathize with me at this point, being already wet himself. I'm just glad I didn't bring any of my expensive blankets.

"Come out here."

I open the door and it's pouring. There is no way I am going out in that, and now the water is already starting to pool inside my tent. "Get in here," I say, grabbing him by his shirt, pulling him inside. "Holy crap!" I scream. His wet clothes against my bare arm are freezing. "Are you crazy?"

"Yup," he says, smiling, moving in to kiss me. I put my hands on his chest, which is soaked through.

"You're going to get us in so much trouble," I whisper.

"Maybe. Do you want me to leave?" he asks.

I shake my head and he leans forward to kiss me again.

"Riley?" he asks softly.

"You got up and left with her," I say, just as softly.

"What? Who?"

I give him a look.

"Jenny?"

"Of course Jenny," I say and then I wait. I have a million questions, the biggest being: Did you kiss her? And I don't want to ask, because if this were normal-Riley, if he kissed her in the

139

woods tonight I wouldn't kiss him tonight, or ever again. But this isn't normal-Riley. This is nature-infected-Riley and I'm terrified of asking, because if he says, *Yes, I kissed her,* I might still want to kiss him.

"Nothing happened, Riley," he says, leaning back to look me in the face. He is still so close that I could feel my eyes cross, and so I close my eyes.

"Why not?"

"Because she's not the one I want something to happen with," he says, bending his face down again, until his cheek is against mine. He moves his hand around me, and I jump again as his wet sleeve hits my arm.

"In the full interest of keeping this platonic," he says, looking at me and smiling, "I'm asking permission. But can I take off my shirt? I'm absolutely freezing and —"

"Go ahead," I say. He pulls his shirt over his head and I can't really see — but I run my hand along his shoulder. He's got a scar line on the back of his right shoulder. I run a fingertip back and forth across it while he sucks in a breath. "What's this from?"

"Falling off my bike in the fifth grade," he says. "I was a late learner. My dad . . . well, he was still around then, he was teaching me and let go, and I wasn't ready."

"Oh," I say, not quite knowing what to say. I think about the scar and wonder about his parents, who — I guess — put this kid together. I wonder who his dad was to counteract the woman I knew to be his mother.

Eric flops down on the blanket covering the bottom of my tent. I am half on top of him, a little bit awkward, and when I try to settle with my weight off of him more, it doesn't quite work. He pulls me onto him, snuggling me under the crook of his arm. "You're not against snuggling, are you?"

"Um, I don't know," I say, trying to get comfortable. He laughs and I pinch his side lightly, feeling the muscles twitch under my touch.

"Any reason to touch me."

I pinch him again.

"When did you learn?"

"Hmm?" I ask, touching the muscles that are bunching under his skin. It is strange to feel them there. His body is so different from mine, which has a soft pillowy feel to it. His is hard and tight, coiled almost, and I begin to wonder if he wonders the same thing when he touches me. His hand is rubbing across my stomach and over my hip. I tense up. What does he think when he touches me? Is he thinking about how much I weigh? How different our bodies are?

"When did you learn how to ride a bike?"

Or does he think about bike riding?

"I never learned."

"What?" he says, his head popping up as he goes onto an

elbow so he can look me in the face, for as much as the darkness would allow us to see.

"I mean, what for? I wasn't priming to be a bike messenger."

"For fun, Swain. For fun," he says. I smile in the darkness at the use of my last name. It's such a pet-name thing to do. "Don't worry, I'll teach you how. And I won't let go."

Suddenly I bristle. His hand is kneading my side at the hip a little. He's using pet names, he's talking about the future. Our future.

"Too much?" he asks.

"Kind of," I say, pulling his hand off my skin, where it has lurked under my shirt a little. I hold it there. "We haven't really talked about what'll happen when I go home and . . ."

"And I'm talking like we're already partners for life," he says, and sighs. Then he pulls his hand away and puts it back on my hip. "Look, I'm just excited to know you. And whatever this is, for however long it is for, I'm just saying . . . I'm happy that I'm in it."

"No pressure?" I ask.

Instead of answering me, he smiles and kisses me, and whatever is left of my brain pools at the base of my spine and collects in a nice warm puddle.

The rain is sprinkling overhead, it's late, we talk and laugh and kiss all night long. When it gets really late, so late that it starts looking like it's getting to be really, really early, we start talking about him leaving. Every time we do, we snuggle together a little more. Our brains are functioning; our bodies aren't complying.

I want to put this out there, because I know it's going to be important for some people, especially those who think they know me, or think they know guys, or think they know how this sort of thing goes. I want to put it out there that we didn't have sex. Not because he didn't ask. He asked. And not because I didn't want to, because there were times when I was only two more questions away from a yes.

But it just felt right to say no, and it just felt right for him to say OK, and go on snuggling — but it was hard. Ha-ha, that's a bad joke, but it was *difficult* to say no. Especially when I didn't want to say no. But when I did, it was at least partially just to see how he'd react.

Sometimes I think he must be too good to be true. And that the real Eric will just come out whenever I least expect it. And isn't the best time to learn about a guy when he wants to have sex and you say no? For whatever reason?

He didn't push me, he was really OK with me saying no. And the minute I realized that, I *really* wanted to say yes (really, really!).

Perhaps it was all part of his evil plan, like reverse psychology.

Maybe it's as simple as that.

143

Maybe he really likes me.

Maybe I want him more than sleep.

We both fall asleep an hour after sunrise. Unfortunately, neither of us wakes up before the rest of the camp.

Eric bends over me and kisses me, and I try to keep my lips tightly pressed against each other (morning breath), but I slowly ease up and we are making out again five seconds later.

"Kids do like their kissing," he says, smiling against my mouth.

"They do, don't they?" I say, kissing him again. I feel like I am still sleeping. Dreamy and kissing in the morning.

Sam is the first person to give my tent a kick. That wakes us up. We both give each other worried looks. Eric whispers, "OK, we just have to wait until everyone shoves off. I'll make a run for it. Back to the van."

"The van is out there?! Don't you think that they'll see it and wonder where the driver is?" OK, I'm freaking out, but give me a little credit. This is freak-out worthy.

"How else do you think I got here? Plus, I don't think that they are going to see my van and say, 'Quick, he's in Riley's tent, let's get him!'" he says, skimming his hands around the tent for his shirt.

"Watch the wandering hands, mister!"

"Sorry. I'm looking for my shirt."

"I can't believe you're doing this at a time —"

"Riley?"

"Shhh," Eric says, his hand over my mouth.

"Riley, are you okay?" I pull Eric's fingers off of my face.

"Yes, I'm fine. A little under the weather," I say as Eric shakes his head wildly and then groans, his head falling back.

"Oh, no," Sam says from the other side of the tent. "I'll grab Ms. Barnell."

Oh. Oops.

"Nice work," he says, suddenly having found his shirt.

"Well, I was under a lot of pressure!" I say, moving to tickle him. He barks a laugh before he is able to move my hands from his hips. Oops, really ticklish.

"Riley?" Sergeant Bullwhip is outside the tent now.

Eric and I both pause. If she only knew. "Yes?" I try and croak. How does one sound when they are sick enough to be left alone, but not so sick that they need someone to come into their tent and rescue them? That's what I'm going for. It apparently doesn't work.

"Riley, come out here right now, please."

"Um, I've got cramps. I think I got my period. I can't move," I say. Eric makes a face. I make a face back. This is his fault. I only use *female problems* in really stressful situations. It's better than my aunt died and I can't leave my tent because I'm grieving.

145

"Ms. Swain, come out now, please."

"*Merde!*" I say, backing my ass out of the tent, Eric making faces at me the entire way, me making growly faces back at him.

I crawl out of the tent and turn to face Sergeant Bullwhip, glad that I had the presence of mind to keep all my clothing on.

"Ms. Swain," she says, pointing to the side. I move over. I look around and only Samantha stands there, looking confused. "Mr. Hotra, you may come out as well."

There isn't any movement from the tent.

"Now, Mr. Hotra," she says, in the same voice that caused me to start doing jumping jacks. Apparently it works on teen boys as well, because Eric comes out about the same way I did, except shirtless. I hear Samantha gasp.

Sergeant Bullwhip doesn't look surprised.

"Ms. Swain, Mr. Hotra, please go to the headmistress's office." Eric groans, but Sergeant Bullwhip snaps a look at him. "Samantha will go with you. You will explain why I sent you both there. When we return from our hike, I'll join you."

Crap.

The ride back to the grounds is unusually quiet. I sit in the backseat with Samantha. Eric didn't hold the door open for us (it was motorized anyway), and we sit there, sending each other long, worried glances. Her glances say:

Are you freaking crazy?

Mine back say: *Um.*

146

Hers say: *What the hell were you doing with him?*
Mine back say: *Um.*
Hers: *Why did he have his shirt off?*
Mine: *Um.*
Hers: *Did you . . .*
Mine: (shaking head madly) *No!*
Hers: *I believe you.*
Mine: *We did some other . . .*
Hers: *OMG. I don't believe you!*
Mine: *(smug smile)*
Hers: *(smile and eye roll)*

Too bad Eric misses all the fun by having his eyes glued to the road. There is absolute silence, not even the radio to alleviate the oppressive quiet.

When we get back (which takes way longer than it should have, thank you, Eric), Samantha walks into the building with us, and when the secretary sees us all, she smiles and greets Samantha and Eric warmly and introduces herself to me. She hadn't been there the other night when I arrived. She has us wait outside when we ask to see Eric's mom.

In case you are wondering, there *is* something infinitesimally embarrassing about admitting to an authority figure that you got caught making out with your not-quite-boyfriend in your tent, on a camping trip, in the middle of what's supposed to be a punishment-style-fat-flush spring break.

Now add to that another one hundred percent embarrassment for having to confess in front of the boy you made out with.

Now add to that another one hundred percent embarrassment for having to confess to the boy-in-question's mother.

Merde.

"Eric? Ms. Swain? To what do I owe the pleasure of having you both here in my office this morning?" she says from behind her desk, after letting Samantha leave. Lucky. I would gladly slink through the extra-wide wooden planks before admitting —

"Ms. Barnell caught me in Riley's tent this morning," Eric says, smiling at his mother.

"Excuse me?"

"Last night after the girls went to sleep, I drove back up the hill and snuck into Riley's tent. We didn't do anything but talk and kiss" (he lies, but only a little — and I respect white lies) "and then we fell asleep. I didn't mean to get caught there, and I'm sorry. I didn't mean to get her into trouble —"

"Eric, stop," I say. "It's not his fault. I could've — I mean, I should've —"

"That's enough," Eric's mother says. "Ms. Swain, please go down to the BC. I'll call in a moment to let her know why you are there. I, outrageously, feel ill-equipped to handle this particular scenario. But I hope you will rest assured that there will be repercussions for your behavior."

"Mom."

"For the both of you."

Wow.

"You may go, Ms. Swain."

My maybe-boyfriend's mother hates me. He's looking at me like he's really upset that I'm really upset and I hate that he's upset.

"Eric," I say kinda loudly, my eyes on him, although I can see Mrs. Hotra's lips purse in the corner of my eyes. "Last night was wonderful."

I leave as he laughs and his mother gasps. If you're going to get in trouble, might as well do *something* worth getting in trouble for. I mean, beyond sneaking a boy into your tent and . . . well, you know.

BACK ON THE COUCH

I'm back in Katie Wilhelm's office. She's not here yet, so I'm walking around the office, looking again at the framed pictures she has around. There are a bunch of different ones. Her with different girls who must have gone through the program, because they are at varying stages of fat.

I wonder which girl I look like as I glance through the pictures. I mean, aside from having the most amazing breasts in the world (yes, we know!), do I look like this girl physically? Do I think she's fat? Do I think other people see this when they look at me, or do they look for more?

I move on to the next picture. The girl standing next to Ms. Wilhelm looks happy. She's not fat; she's not thin. She's just smiling and radiant. She's wearing face paint.

The next picture, a girl's crying.

The next picture, a bunch of girls are surrounding Ms. Wilhelm.

The next. The next. The next. There are a lot of pictures of girls around the room, and if I was any kind of psychological

150

student, I'd say that Ms. Wilhelm needs a whole lot of positive reinforcement. Or, she's just plain old freaky.

On the top shelf, all the way to the right, in the corner, is another picture. It's black-and-white, a school photo. A young girl wearing a cap and gown, but her cheeks are gaunt and she's got deep circles under her eyes. I take the picture down so I can get a better look at it. It looks like Ms. Wilhelm, but her hair is thinner-looking and she doesn't look happy; she looks tired and old.

"That was me at age twenty-one. I weighed ninety-seven pounds. My healthy weight range was one hundred twenty to one hundred thirty pounds for my height. Two weeks after that photo was taken, my parents convinced me to check into a reha-bilitation clinic for malnutrition and anorexia," Ms. Wilhelm says, walking in behind me. She takes the photo from my hands and puts it back on the top shelf.

"So you were a thin girl."

"I was an unhealthy girl, Riley."

"And now you've devoted your life to becoming the girl who helps fat girls get thin. You don't think that's a little twisted?"

"I like to think of it as having devoted my life to helping girls, all girls, get healthy."

"And you consider me unhealthy?"

"Riley, look, you're not physically unhealthy. You're not

151

obese, you're a little overweight. You don't have any weight-related health problems. You don't have any issues that I'm concerned about at this point," she says, but before I have a chance to feel good about her admission, she starts again. "But your medical history shows that there are a lot of weight-related medical problems in your family tree. Your father —"

"My father?"

"Yes, your father says that he's worried about you."

"Ha, that's rich."

"What? That your father could be worried about you?" She motions for the chair, and I sit down in a huff as she sits gracefully behind her desk.

"Well, considering he hasn't talked to me more than two sentences in the past year, and that's with his BlackBerry in hand, I wouldn't say he's too worried."

"You feel like he doesn't pay enough attention to you," she says, marking something in her notebook.

"I'm not saying that. I'm saying he doesn't pay any attention to me at all."

"Is that why you feel the need to get attention from other men?"

Oh. I see. Tricky.

"Not really."

"Do you think your behavior with Eric was appropriate?" she asks.

"I think it was appropriate enough. I mean, if I were a guy,

152

would anyone be asking if this was appropriate or would this be fine because I was a guy and this is the sort of thing that guys do? And furthermore, nothing happened. Nothing happened, nothing happened."

"Riley," she says, leaning forward in her seat, so that her arms are crossed over her chest on her desk blotter. "Something happened. Whether or not it was sex is another story. Whether or not you used protection — even if nothing happened, as you say — there are things that happened."

"I don't know."

"You don't know what?"

"I don't know why it matters," I huff back, a little angry that she is trying to be all high and mighty. Nothing happened, and I can't understand why nobody will believe me. Well, of course I can understand . . . I guess it makes sense, but come on, even if something did happen . . . it is really none of her business.

"It matters because I worry about what's going to happen to you."

"Ha."

"Riley, it's OK to be upset," she says, and for the first time, I realize that I'm crying. Which is really ridiculous. I'm *angry*, not upset. I tell her so, and she just repeats the same line again. It's OK to be upset. Like I'm even supposed to know what that means.

"You're an amazing girl, Riley. You deserve attention, but the right kind of attention. No, don't roll your eyes. You do. You deserve a lot of things. I want you to think about that when you're back in your room. Take the rest of the day off."

"What?"

"I'm telling Mrs. Hotra that you'll be taking the rest of the day off to think about your actions."

"That's it?"

"Oh no, you've also earned yourself another demerit. One more strike and you're out of here. Do we understand each other?"

I sniffle, feeling relieved, for whatever reason. I don't want to go home just yet.

"Yes." I nod.

"OK, go back to your room."

"What happens to Eric?"

"He will *not* be going back to your room."

I gave her a scowl.

"I'm sure you'll find out soon enough, but I feel bad for him. . . . This can't be a comfortable thing to talk to his mother about."

I nod again and head back to my room. Thinking about what Ms. Wilhelm said, I'm not sure any of it makes sense but, well, I have all day to think about it.

SAMANTHA GOES CRAZY

When I get back to our room, Samantha is there waiting there for me, looking worried.

"What happened?" she asks as I flop back onto my bed and hear something creak hideously beneath me. I miss my old bed. I miss my old room. I miss the comfort of knowing that everyone is a liar and a jerk and being able to move effortlessly through that social world because I could be a liar and a jerk too. I don't know this world.

"Nothing," I say, blinking at the ceiling.

"Nothing?"

"I've been sent to my room to think about what I've done."

"What?" Samantha screeches. I look over at her and she looks seriously pissed off.

"I mean, I got a demerit-thingy too."

"You make out with the only boy on campus, you get caught with him in your tent, God knows you probably had sex with him —"

"Hey now!"

155

"And your punishment for all of this is that you get to spend the rest of the day in air-conditioning while I'm out there skipping and eating gruel and dealing with all those absolute bitches?"

"Absolute bitches and Allie."

"I already included her!"

I cough a little. She seems really pissed off. She used the word *bitches*.

"I don't really understand why you are upset," I say in my most dulcet tone. I wonder if I should start singing to her, like they do with angry animals to calm them down, but the only lyrics that come to mind are for Michael Jackson's "Thriller" and I'm so not in the mood for that right now. "But I'd like to talk about it with you and see if we can't resolve this before it becomes an even bigger issue."

She snorts. Hey, I tried.

"I just don't appreciate the fact that I'm always good," Samantha fumes. "I mean, I always, *always* behave, I'm always a good person. I never argue, I turn the other cheek — dammit! And you come in here and kick and bitch and make problems and you get the boy *and* a vacation."

"This isn't necessarily what I'd consider a vacation," I say, looking around the room.

"It isn't fair."

"I never said you couldn't get in trouble," I mumble.

"I know you didn't," she says, flopping back onto her bed too. Now we match. Now we both feel defeated by who we are and what this place brings out in us. Great.

My phone begins buzzing and it takes me a few moments to find it among the clothing that was all over the floor (oops). My "A little help here?" goes unheeded by Samantha, who simply picks up her pillow and covers her face with it. Well, then.

I am so excited to get my fingers wrapped around the phone before it has a chance to switch to voice mail that I pressed the ON button, and say in a rush, "I'm so glad you called. What happened? Are you in trouble?"

"What do you mean am *I* in trouble?"

"D?" I ask, pulling the phone away long enough to see that, yes, it is his name registering on my caller ID.

"Who did you think it was?"

"Nobody," I say, sitting on the bed again, watching Samantha peek an eye out from underneath her pillow. I turn around on the bed so that I'm facing the wall. I hear her huff, but I'm concentrating — or trying to — on what D is saying to me.

"Where are you?"

"In the rec room," I lie. Samantha looks up and is raising her eyebrows. I make the "not now, later" face. She makes the "fine, whatever" face.

"I just called the front desk and they said there isn't a Riley Swain registered at Dahlia's."

"Why did you call the front desk?"

"Why aren't you registered?" he asks, and finally I realize there is something weird going on. He doesn't sound like his normal, laid-back self. There is a long pause and we're both waiting for each other to talk. Does he know? Does he know I lied to him?

"What's the matter?" I ask.

"Your voice mail, for starters."

Oh. I had forgotten about that. That seems like forever ago. I mean, so much has happened since then that I can't even think about it as if it was a recent thing. It's weird, now that I know that I'm not in love with D, our conversations feel different.

Like, I'm not under his spell anymore and so I don't mind that he's upset and I'm not immediately jumping up to soothe his ruffled feathers.

"Something's different," he says softly, sounding hurt, and I begin to feel bad. He's my best friend, isn't he? Or have I been using his friendship as a way to stay close to him because I liked him and wanted him as more than a friend?

"D —" I begin. I'm not sure what I'm going to say, but I think it's important to say something here. Perhaps there is a chance to start again. To try to be friends as friends should be. And not what we were.

"No, don't say anything," he says. He sounds tired and upset. "I'm going to visit you. I'll be there Saturday."

"What?"

"I'm coming to pick you up and take you back to the city."

"Yes, but —"

"OK, then, I'll pick you up. I'll be there Saturday and we'll talk about all of this then," he says. "And, Riley?"

"Hmm?" I strangle out.

"Whatever is going on, it's OK. I mean, you're my best friend in the entire world and we'll fix this. I'll fix this. I really love you, you know?"

"I know, D," I say, and I mean it. It was never really a question of whether he loved me as a friend. I guess I always knew that. I guess it was just a matter of why he couldn't love me as more or why I couldn't love him as less. Until now.

I click off the phone and I turn around to face Samantha, when my phone starts buzzing again. I look down and open the text message from Marley:

Busted. C U soon.

"That sounded . . . interesting. What's going on?"

"I'm an asshole and an idiot!" I scream, throwing the phone across the room. Then I tell her the entire story. About how D kissed me before I left and how I don't know what that means because we haven't had a chance to talk about it. How I realize I don't love him. How I realize I might, in fact, love Eric. How my dad doesn't care. How Ms. Wilhelm thinks I'm a slut. How I am a slut because I wanted to sleep with Eric soooo bad. How I'm a virgin —

"Wait, you're a virgin?"

And I tell her about how D is coming up here to pick me up from the "spa," and Marley, who is trying to steal him, and how I am horrible and . . . and . . . and . . .

"Wait, you're a virgin?"

"Can you get *over* that?"

"It's just —"

"What?" I cry. "Do I have *superslut* written across my forehead?"

"No, it's just that you seem so experienced."

"It's because I'm fabulous[3]," I say, tucking my hair behind my ears and wiping the moisture from under my eyes. My God, I'm not wearing any eyeliner. Ugh. "People often mistake fabulous for other things."

"Like full of —"

"Ahem," I say, shaking my head slowly.

She smiles, tucks her red hair behind her ears, and overdramatically blinks a few times before wiping away a fake tear.

"Look, this isn't as bad as you think it is," she says.

"Of course it is. It's *always* as bad as I think it is," I tell her.

---

3. True. Sometimes people will think you are more mature, more experienced, richer and more beautiful, when in reality — you're just more fabulous than they are. Simple rebuttal? I'm not more X, I'm just fabulous. Or, if it's a guy, "I'm not more X, you're just attracted to me."

"Why don't you just tell D that you lied?"

I look at her and roll my eyes. Naive.

"Of course I can't do that!" I say, exasperated. Hasn't she been listening?

"Why not?"

"D . . ." I sit up and pull both my pillows onto my lap. "D's mom cheated on D's dad. But, like, D was the one who caught her."

"Like, *caught her* caught her?" I see Sam's eyes widen.

"Not caught in the heat of passion or anything but, like, he caught her getting out of this town car and he thought he saw something. But she covered it up and told him some lie about it. I'm not really sure exactly what happened; he doesn't talk about it very much. Anyway, she left two weeks later and his dad basically was wrecked."

"And this has to do with you and D how?"

"Well, his big thing is lying. Like, you can do or say anything. Be a horrible person. You can kill his dog, but if you lie to him . . . it's like this unfixable sin."

Sam looks at me, the full weight of the issue (no pun intended) sinking in.

"So why did you lie, then?"

I shake my head a little. "I didn't want him to know that . . . well, I didn't want him to know that my dad was sending me here. I didn't want him to think of me as being the type of person who needed to be here."

161

Sam stiffens, like I knew she would.

"I didn't know what I was talking about."

"No, I understand," she says, bending a little. "The only people who know where I am are my family."

I pause for a moment to think about that. "Can I see the hot pic of your stepbrother?"

"Not a chance," she snaps, but then smiles. "Look, what's the big deal? As long as you're home before D leaves to pick you up — no harm done."

"How can I be home if I'm here?"

I look at her. She nods. I get it. All I have to do is go home. Or rather, all I have to do is get *sent* home.

"OK, listen. I have to go to physical recreation or whatever, but I'll be back and we'll figure this out."

"Thanks, Sam," I say. She gives me a thumbs-up and leaves me alone to freak.

THEBIGUN17: You're online!

RILEDUP: Obviously. Why are you so surprised?

THEBIGUN17: Oh, no reason. What's going on?

RILEDUP: I'm planning my escape from upstate NY.

THEBIGUN17: What?

RILEDUP: I'm going back to the city.

THEBIGUN17: Why? What happened? You didn't get kicked out, did you?

RILEDUP: Not yet, but I'm working on it.

THEBIGUN17: As a purely objective, third-party observer, what about this new guy?

RILEDUP: ::sigh:: I don't know. I'll have to figure that out later. But I can't lose D over this.

THEBIGUN17: You can just call and tell him the truth.

RILEDUP: No, I can't.

WHEN ALL ELSE FAILS, ORDER TAKE-OUT

I need to get sent home. How do I do that?" I ask.

"You're obviously not worried about breaking the rules, so why don't you break one or two more?" Sam suggests. She tucks her feet under her and sits cross-legged on her bed. I notice, for the first time, that she has a rainbow comforter. This girl needs some serious help.

"How do I do that? I mean, how do I do that without getting in trouble with my parents and . . . well, what about Eric?"

"I was thinking about this while doing jumping jacks."

"Jumping jacks?"

"Core strengthening," she says, grimacing.

We've been sitting in our room for a while now with my Hello Kitty notebook, making lists and making plans. I must say, if I were in jail, I'd hope for Sam to be my roommate to help me break out. What am I saying? I am in jail.

"Here's the idea." Sam's face brightens. "We stage an eat-in."

"What? Can't I just push Tilly down a mine shaft and get kicked out for that?"

"Riley," Sam says, sighing. She stands up and goes to her desk and brings back a small pamphlet that I recognize as the New Horizons handbook. She flips it open, looking for something.

Hmm . . . so that's what the inside looks like.

"'Rule Thirteen,'" she reads. "'While temporary on-campus probation might be rendered in lieu of suspension and expulsion for multiple demerits on a case-by-case basis, the confiscation of or possession of items either food or otherwise will necessitate immediate expulsion.'"

"Huh?"

"It means that the only sure way of getting kicked out is by having this food stuff."

I do get it, but . . . "Why an eat-in? Why not just get, like, Krispy Kreme doughnuts and walk around with them dropping out of my pockets?"

"Because I'm sick of being a Goody Two-shoes around here and I want to make a point," she says, snapping the guidebook shut again.

"What point is that?"

"That I have a voice and that I can make up my own mind about what I do and what I eat and . . . and where I go to school."

Uh-oh . . . teenage angst, meet Samantha. Samantha, teen-age angst.

I nod, because who am I to stand in the way of Samantha's newly found mental freedom? We spend the rest of the afternoon (or her forty-two-minute break) planning our eat-in.

The first part of our plan: *Delivering Blacklisted Goods.*

We need to order and have delivered a lot of blacklisted items. The way one orders Chinese in NY.

I need to call Eric, the only person I know on campus who might do this for me. For us.

"But I can't tell him why!"

"Riley, you should just tell him," Samantha says.

She doesn't understand relationships, or men, at all.

I call his number. Mr. Right.

"Eric? It's Riley. . . . I need a favor." I pause; he doesn't respond. "Remember me? The girl you were caught making out with and got a demerit and drove insane with lust and passion?"

"Um, is everything OK?"

"Everything is fine, but I was hoping you could do me a favor," I say.

"Of course, uh — what do you need?"

Samantha is standing over my right shoulder. For no other reason than to keep her from having a major stroke.

I need to get to the point and get there soon.

"Look, I need a dealer," I say, lowering my voice.

"Huh?"

"We're staging a small coup here at New Horizons. I need some stuff and someone on the outside to get said stuff."

"What stuff are we talking about?"

"Oh, I don't know . . . Twinkies. Bagels. Whole milk. Basically anything that has a minimum of twenty-five carbohydrate grams per serving with the majority coming from fat."

"My mom isn't going to like that," he says, his voice hushed.

"That's the point."

"And let's say I help you get the stuff. What are you going to do with it?"

"Does it matter?" I ask.

"Of course it matters," he replies. "I may occasionally work in the black market, but I wouldn't sell a glazed doughnut to a diabetic. I might not have ethics but I definitely have my morals."

"What's the difference?"

"Living by your morals means you abide by what you feel is right or wrong. Living by ethics means you abide by what other people feel is right or wrong."

"And if I swear that no diabetics will be harmed by your actions?"

"Not good enough. I need details or there will be no stuff."

Someone is coming around the corner and Samantha is motioning the kill-sign at me.

"Yes, Aunt DeeDee, I completely understand and I'll be happy to tell you all about it some other time!" I smile as the girl who I recognize from my PE class walks by Samantha and me. We lean against the wall. Samantha pretends to be picking at her cuticles and the girl gives us a funny look and keeps walking. When she gets to the corner, Samantha gives me a look that says, *That was close and we better get out of here!*

"Now, please," was all Eric responds.

I pause, contemplating letting Eric in on our complete scheme.

"We're staging an eat-in."

Samantha's eyes bug out and she makes choking motions with her hands, her tongue sticking out the corner of her mouth. Seriously, she needs to calm that shit down.

I turned around to avoid making eye contact with her.

"An eat-in?"

"You know, like an old-fashioned nonviolent form of pro-test. Like they used in the sixties."

"Isn't that a sit-in?"

"Yes, well, those people were fighting against action with inaction. I'm fighting against being thin-ified by eating."

There is a silence from Eric's end that I find extremely unsettling. I think he might be laughing so hard that he can't breathe and I prepare myself to hear a guffaw at any point. But he doesn't laugh. Not even a chuckle. He simply says, "OK.

E-mail me a list of your needs and when you'll need it by." Then he pauses. "Riley?" he asks.

"Yeah?" I ask, as Samantha pulls on my arm.

"What you're doing . . . what I think you're doing. It's pretty cool."

He always says the right thing, except right now the right thing is the worst thing he possibly could've said. I want to tell him that I want to run away and this is why I am doing this. Instead I just say, "Thanks, I gotta run."

"Oh . . . um . . . absolutely. Talk to you later," he says. I can hear the confusion in his voice, the questions. The "Are we OK?" that is looming, and I'm not sure. I mean, on one hand there are a million reasons why I should love him, but I loved — I mean I love — D and so I can't really love Eric. This is too much.

"I'll e-mail you. Bye," I say, blowing him a kiss and then hanging up.

"He said yes?" Samantha asks.

"He said yes."

I hand her the folded paper with his e-mail address and she looks up at me and smiles. "Phase two?"

I nod. "Phase two."

Phase two is easy. Phase two is just a matter of time and attention. Phase three, on the other hand, necessitates cunning and skilled negotiation. This is where I will shine. This is where my father would have cried, clasped me to his bosom, and muttered, "My daughter, my darling daughter. I know thee, because you are a reflection of me." (Don't ask me where I get this shit. I'm just THAT worldly).

"OK, we need a research party," I say, addressing the entire room. "I need a list of food, pronto, that would head up the twenty-five worst of Mrs. Hotra's deadly sins of food."

"I can do that," Samantha says, raising her hand. "I can Google like mad."

"That's true." Allison nods. "She's practically obsessive-compulsive when it comes to Googling."

"What?" Samantha says, turning in her seat toward Allie. "That's slander!"

"Um . . . remember Thomas?"

Samantha doesn't say a word. She doesn't have to. Blood must've been in a mad rush to get to her cheeks because her face is flooded bright red.

"Who was Thomas?" I ask.

Samantha sends Allie a pleading look. But since I am the only one who asked, it is clear everyone else has heard this story already. I am still out of the loop on some old business, it seems. Would I ever catch up?

"Thomas was this guy who Samantha met at last year's end-of-the-year trip. She was totally into him and he was totally into her" (insert gag sound from Samantha) "and he gave her his e-mail address. And Samantha Googled him and found his MySpace page and basically MySpace-stalked him through a fake profile she created."

"So? That sounds reasonable."

"Thank you, Riley!" Samantha yells.

Allie nods, "Yeah, totally — who hasn't MySpace-stalked someone? But have you ever stalked the people who leave comments on your space only to find out that one is your crush's ex-girlfriend?"

I nod. Totally did that.

"Well, have you ever Googled her only to find out she was, like, some model and then decided that if the guy liked someone like that, he couldn't ever like you?"

I look over at Samantha, whose eyes are down — she is concentrating on her lap. "Look, I know it sounds crazy. I just couldn't understand why . . ."

"Maybe he was sick of pretty, thin girls. . . ." Allie says, snickering.

"Shut up, Allie."

I laugh. Old news. Same news. But no, I never thought that. I guess I take it for granted that guys like me. Guys love a girl with big . . . well, we've been here before. But I guess I can see what Sam was worried about. It's hard not to compare your-self to those around you. Even at fat school, it's like, who is the fattest among the fat girls? Who has the most fashion sense? The scale might be slightly skewed, but the game is still the same. We are all still making the comparisons.

"I once pretended to be someone else on IM and started talk-ing to a boyfriend to see if he would be open to cheating on me."

Allie looks over, but Samantha is the one who asks, "Was he?"

"Of course. I was talking like such a ho."

"Did you dump him?"

"In the end, I couldn't . . . I mean, I couldn't really blame him for dumping me so he could have me, now could I? Sure, he was a dick for potentially cheating on me, but he was going to do so to be with . . . me."

"That's screwed up, Riley."

"Can I blame a man for wanting me? In any incarnation? No . . . he shouldn't be punished for being too weak to with-stand my power!" I say standing in the middle of the room with my hands above my head — power pose. I am like a chubbed-out superheroine.

"Riley," Allie asks, turning off David Bowie for a minute.

"What's up?" I say, plopping down on the bed next to her.

"Why are you leaving?"

"Because if I don't, D is going to find out I lied to him," I say, getting up and giving her one of those "are you silly?"

looks. But Sam is looking at me the same way Allie is, and I feel like my answer wasn't good enough, so I plop down on the floor, my back against the bed frame, so I can look at both of them.

"I'm not sure you should be doing this for a guy you can't even be honest with," says Sam.

"What do you mean?"

"I mean, let's look at this analytically," she says. "How good of friends can you be if you can't even tell him where you are? What are you getting out of this so-called friendship?"

"Well, he's my best friend," I say, kicking my feet out from under me as I begin to lose feeling in my toes.

"Yeah, but you wanted more than that." Sam cuts me off when I'm about to argue. "Not now, of course, but before. If he really loved you like you say he does," she goes on, "he'll understand and you don't need to go through all of this."

Sam and Allie look at me all expectantly.

I look at them and then away again. "What if I was only friends with him because I wanted him to love me? What kind of friend can I possibly be? What if I don't really love him? I can't imagine what it would be like not loving him. He's my best friend. No, no — I mean it. My dad forgot my birthday."

Allie gasps.

"And I thought maybe he was playing around, like it was coming later, or there was a surprise or something. And so I didn't say anything, I just waited and waited. And it never came. He just forgot."

"That's horrible," Sam says.

"I mean, whatever." I shrug.

"No, that's horrible. You must have felt horrible," she says.

"Yeah." I nod. "I did."

"But," I continue, "D called me later that night after I had seen him at school and I guess I sounded miserable, because he told me to get dressed right away, and he came and picked me up. I snuck out of the house and he took me out, and we spent all night out having fun and it was the most amazing night of my life."

"And?"

"And nothing. He made me feel like it didn't matter that my dad forgot my birthday," I say. "He always does stuff like that. He doesn't *love me*, but he loves me. And I can't let him find out that I lied to him about this . . . ever. I mean, I must love him enough to want to keep him from finding out that I lied. . . ."

There are a few minutes of silence before Samantha says, "You have to tell Eric the whole truth about the plan." (I nod.) "And about D. Just be honest with him, Riley. He'll understand. He'll want to."

THE PLAN

D is planning on driving upstate with Marley on Saturday. Which means that I have to be back in Manhattan by Saturday morning at the latest.

My dad and Elizabitch are going to the Hamptons for the weekend. They are leaving on Friday night. Since my dad is a creature of habit, I assume that they will leave at the same time they've left for the past six months: seven P.M.

I would flip the call-forwarding at the house at 7:05 P.M., and then stage the eat-in, which would give me (and Samantha — it was her idea for the eat-in, she says, and so she has to be included. Plus it would only be her first demerit ever) my third demerit and automatic suspension.

A call home would be forwarded to my cell phone, which Samantha and Allie would be handling. I would get kicked out, make the ten P.M. train back to the city, and arrive with enough time to call and reroute D.

*   *   *

175

"What are you going to tell your dad?" Sam asks as we hunker down in Allie's room.

"If he even notices? Um, I haven't figured that out yet."

"They *are* going to notice when you're home a week earlier than they expected," Sam points out.

"I always have the option of going on the Mexico trip, and then I'll be getting home at the same time that I'd be getting home from New Horizons, and they may never know."

Allie just shakes her head while Sam looks dubious.

"I'll figure that part out when it comes to it," I say.

Eric had text-messaged me that the food was on its way so we go downstairs to the back door just as he is pulling in.

"Hey," he says, smiling at me. He nods and waves at Allie and Sam, who are both smirking at us. They each take a bag and then Sam says loudly, "Let's let them alone for a couple of minutes so Riley can talk to Eric. Riley, don't forget we have workshop in twenty minutes."

Workshop, oh yeah — how to cook without fat. Sweet.

"Thanks, yeah."

They leave us alone.

"Do you have something you need to tell me?" Eric asks, looking at me questioningly. I kick my toe at an imaginary pebble. I am conscious of all things. How close he is standing. How close he isn't standing. How my thigh muscles feel (as I kick said imaginary pebble). How cold the wind is (and I wonder if I

176

have hard nipples). And of course — how much there was not being said.

"Yeah, um. Yes."

"What is it?"

"I kind of didn't tell you the whole story behind what's going on," I say, shuffling my feet. I'm wearing these really cute ballerina slippers in red plaid. I've noticed that I stopped wearing heels. But it has nothing to do with Eric, really.

"What's the whole story?"

"I'm trying to get kicked out," I tell him, "of New Horizons."

"Were you going to tell me or would I have just found all this out after you had already left?" He's really calm, but I can tell he's upset.

"I didn't know how to tell you."

"Why? Why do this?"

"I — I have to go home. I don't fit in here. I need to go home," I say, floundering. I don't want to tell him about D. I don't want him to think it's not because I don't like him, or that I like D more. It's like apples and oranges. Or Twinkies and Ho Hos. Or rather, Oreos or cheesecake from Junior's in Brooklyn?

The door opens behind us and I see Eric's face as he looks over his shoulder before I turn around. Jenny is standing behind us.

"Eric?" she asks.

Eric sighs. I get pissed off.

"What do you *want*?" I snap, spinning toward her.

She ignores me and keeps her eyes on Eric. "Eric, I know what she asked you to do. She's going to get you into trouble."

"Jenny . . ." he says.

"No, she's not worth it," Jenny says. "Look, I know, I know we made some mistakes."

"Holy crap!" I say. "Are you kidding me? Can you get lost? You can try and get him back later tonight — after I'm gone."

"Gone?" she asks.

"Riley —" Eric starts.

"Yes, I'll be gone tonight. OK? You can retract your claws and stop. I'd be gone sooner, but eight is the earliest I could manage. Does that fit into your schedule?"

She gives me a look that I can't read, or perhaps I'm not trying because I'm still concentrating on Eric, whose look I *can* read and it isn't pretty.

"Eric . . ." I say.

"No, forget it. You girls are crazy. I'm out," he says, getting back into the minivan, slamming the door shut, and driving off.

"You shouldn't get him involved," she says. "You'll get him in trouble with his mother."

I raise my eyebrows at her. "I think you should mind your own business."

"He is my business."

I roll my eyes and walk back into the building, letting the door slam behind me as I walk slowly up the stairs.

ON TIME IS LATE, LATE IS UNACCEPTABLE

THEBIGUN17: What?

RILEDUP: ??? What's your problem? My life is falling apart, please don't bail on me too?!

THEBIGUN17: :/ How is your life falling apart — you seem to have a handle on everything and everyone.

RILEDUP: I screwed up.

THEBIGUN17: The great Riley screwed up?

RILEDUP: Yeah . . . I mean, with this guy. The one I've been telling you about.

THEBIGUN17: . . .

RILEDUP: I like him.

THEBIGUN17: You just decided?

RILEDUP: Not just.

THEBIGUN17: Tell him.

RILEDUP: How?

THEBIGUN17: Call him. Tell him. He'll forgive you.

RILEDUP: Promise?

THEBIGUN17: Ha. Yeah, I promise.

The timing of all of this has to be perfect.

I need to buy my ticket home. I have to get "caught" with the food between the hours of seven and eight so I can catch the train before ten P.M. I would call the phone company and get the calls forwarded to my cell phone, which Samantha would be answering and pretending to be Elizabitch. (She is already hyperventilating about her "part" in my so-called crime, but every time I suggest that she try something else, she just snaps that she can handle it and she isn't the Goody Two-shoes that everyone thinks she is. "Uh-huh," says Allie, but another sharp look from Samantha shuts her up too.)

Samantha-cum-Elizabitch would tell Mrs. Hotra that I am a horrible child who needs to be disciplined at home. And she would have a ticket waiting for me. I would be driven to the train station after a teary-eyed good-bye, and I would arrive home, where I would sneak back into my apartment, meet up with D, and go on the trip to Mexico or . . . stay home . . . or . . . whatever. I would figure it out later.

Of course, there are some small gaps of logic in my very reasonable, very sneaky plan to save my social life from ultimate destruction.

"Why don't you come back?" Allie asks.

"I don't see how I can," I say, sitting on the top of my bag, hoping to squish it down long enough to get it zipped, pulling the zipper around it tight.

"What about Eric?" Samantha asks.

I look at her. "I don't know if Eric cares."

"Riley."

"I'm serious. You didn't see how he was looking at me. He wanted nothing to do with me."

"He was hurt," she says, coming over and zipping the zipper up the last few inches for me.

"He was hurt? And that makes everything he said OK? I don't think so," I say. She's about to respond but I cut her off. "Listen, I have enough to worry about — I don't want to think about him right now too."

"Fine," she says, turning away.

"Fine."

"Fine," says Allie. She shrugs when we look at her. "I wanted to feel involved."

When the packing is done, I stick the suitcase underneath my bed and look at my two friends. They look more than a little sad to see me going. It's sweet. Kids do like getting attached. *Eric.*

"All right, then," I start, "everything seems ready."

"Yeah."

"Yeah."

"What do we do now?"

"Well, where's the food?"

"Under the bed," Sam says, sitting on her bed and looking between her ankles at the boxes we've got stacked there.

"OK, suitcases are a check."

"Right."

"And now we just have to buy the ticket and then wait."

"Right," I say, pulling out my wallet and my pretty little credit card. I go online and type in the pertinent details but when I click SUBMIT, it bounces back with an error message. I try it again — same message. What is going on here?

"Riley, it says your card is declined," Sam says, reading over my shoulder.

"What? What do you mean?" I say, looking at her.

"Declined. It says the card has been closed."

I grab the card from her and look at the dates. The card hasn't expired.

"Oh shit," I say. "I've never had this happen before."

"Huh?"

"I might've charged something kind of expensive . . . oh shit . . . they closed my account! Can they do that? Can they just close my account without telling me? Is that even *legal*?"

Samantha shrugs and Allie suggests quietly, "Well, if you went over your limit, I guess."

"Limit? What's a limit?" I scream, kicking the corner of my bed a few times. Now what? Now what? I can't think, so I start pacing.

"I mean, why is it so important that you go home?" Sam speaks up. "Maybe this is a sign that you should stay here with us. It's only another week anyway."

I look over at her and she looks kind of hopeful. How

can I tell her that she's nothing like my friends, and not — technically — my type when it comes to friends or people that I hang out with. How can I tell her that I'm not exactly sure now what I feel about D and that I need to get back there to see him face-to-face to figure it out or I'll never know. I don't know where to begin.

"Don't say anything," Samantha says, giving me a teary smile. "You just want to go home. It has nothing to do with us."

"Right," I lie.

"Right," we all say at the same time, our voices hushed.

"You can use my card," Samantha says, running to her desk and bringing back a small baggie that has a number of credit cards with her name on them. "My dad worries about me. He wants me to feel like I can come home anytime I want to."

"Wow, nice dad."

She shrugs and hands me a card.

"You won't get in trouble for using this?" I ask, holding the card up, suddenly conscious, for the first time, that credit isn't free. Even if it had always felt that way.

"Not at all. It's a prefilled card, so there is no statement."

Sweet.

There is a knock at the door and I shove the card in my back pocket as Samantha throws the other cards into the closet and Allie runs in a small circle screeching, "Oh my God! Oh my God! Oh my God! Oh my God! Someone's at the door!"

"No shit, Sherlock. Open it."

Allie opens the door and shrieks a little. The door pushes open — a hand on the knob revealing Mrs. Hotra and Jenny. Of course.

"Ms. Swain, can I see you in the hallway, please?"

I nod and give Samantha a look that says: *Keep her quiet and calm her down.* Or conversely, *Help.*

I'm out in the hallway with a smug-looking Jenny and Mrs. Hotra. Mrs. Hotra looks tired, perhaps tired of Jenny. I know I am. Rotten, no-good, completely infantile tattletale. I wish I could pull her hair out by the long blond ponytail.

"Ms. Swain, someone has suggested" (someone, whatever — it is completely obvious who the "someone" is) "that you have some material that is not allowed on campus in your possession."

I look down at my hands and pat down my front, as if to say, *No blacklisted items on my person, ma'am.* I try to give her my best confused look. She just sighs again — why does everyone sigh like this around me? All I know is that I can't get kicked out right now. If I get kicked out now, my parents will be called — and they'll still receive the message. I'll be in deep —

"It's not on her, but she definitely has it, Mrs. Hotra," screeches Jenny.

"I don't know what you're talking about."

"Yes you do, you little liar!" Jenny continues to screech at a higher and higher pitch.

"Why don't you just go search my room if that's what you think," I say, bluffing. And for a moment I think I'll get away with it — Mrs. Hotra looks unsure.

"That will not be necessary, Ms. Swain —"

"Fine, I will!" Jenny says, pushing past me and opening the door. She storms into the room, pausing to spin in a circle, around and around. As if a pile of food with which to get me kicked out would suddenly appear and make itself known. Mrs. Hotra steps in behind her.

"Jennifer, where is this food that you suspected Riley had in her possession?"

"Well, um . . ." She looks under my bed. In the closet. "It's not here. But she did have it."

"How do you know that?" Mrs. Hotra is really starting to look annoyed now. Samantha and Allie look from each of us, like a three-way Ping-Pong match. I glance under the bed too — there isn't a box to be found. Not a Kit Kat, not a Ho Ho.

"Jennifer?"

I can see Jenny struggling. Obviously she wants to get me into trouble and out of New Horizons, but not at the cost of having Eric be mad at her. I am counting on her love for him to get me through this. She loves Eric and she would never get him in trouble with his own mother. This will go away and she will have to admit defeat.

"Mrs. Hotra, I saw Eric helping her get it. He delivered it and I saw . . ."

I see her struggle to mention Allie and Samantha. Not like she just didn't get Eric in trouble, but at least she seems to have some sort of conscience.

"And I saw her bring it inside."

I can see the stone wall fall over Mrs. Hotra's face and emotions. She isn't annoyed anymore, she's pissed off now. Swell. I hope they don't find the food now. Wherever it is. I could probably get Eric out of this, but only if they don't find the food. I mean, it's Jenny's word against mine. Who would you believe?

"Ms. Swain, do you have any food in your room?" she asks.

"No," I say, and it's the truth. At least, I think it is.

"Ms. Swain . . . I'd like to see you in my office in half an hour. Please bring your belongings with you."

Well. I guess that settles that question.

Jenny looks satisfied as Mrs. Hotra turns on her heel and stalks out the door, leaving the four of us staring at one another.

"You're going to get what you deserve," Jenny says finally.

"You're an idiot," I say.

"Excuse me?" she repeats.

"You are an idiot. Do I need to dumb it down a shade for you?"

"How *dare* you speak to me that way? I'm not the one who is breaking all the rules and . . . and . . ."

"And kissing your ex-boyfriend! Well, listen to me . . . you lost him. You gave him up. You dumped him."

She shakes her head, but her mouth just keeps gaping open and then slamming shut again. She looks like a swollen, blond-ponytailed codfish. "You dumped him," I continue, "because you didn't know what a great guy you had. He's perfect. He's amazing and everything that a girl could ask for. And now that you realize what you had, you think you can just get him back, like he's going to do your bidding. And what's worse, you don't even like him."

"I do," she says, looking down at her hands. "I do like him."

"No you don't," I tell her. "I like him."

"You don't."

I say it again because it feels good to say. "I like him. I may even love him."

"If you loved him you wouldn't be leaving, you wouldn't have pushed him away," she tells me.

It is completely unfair of her to turn her logic on me. I shrug. "That's between Eric and me. It has nothing to do with you and we'll work it out in our own time."

Her face, which had looked sad with longing a moment ago, begins to scrunch up again once more. "Well, that's just fine. . . . It's obvious why he likes you anyway."

"Oh yeah?" I ask. I'm dying to hear this. What could she possibly say —

"Of course it's obvious. I mean, we dated until I got thin. Obviously he's not into thin girls." (I hear Allie gasp in the background.) "He has a thing for fat chicks."

Awkward silence.

Crickets cricketing.

Silence . . . *la, la, la,* this is silence.

"And —" she starts again, advancing on me.

"That is enough!" Samantha yells. We all stop in our tracks, even Jenny — who turns to her, mouth agape. "Who do you think you are?"

"Excuse me?"

"Who do you think you are, you self-righteous, spoiled, conceited prig?"

"Excuse me!"

"How dare you come in here, into our room, and not only insult Riley, who has never done anything more than make out with your ex-boyfriend — yes, *ex*-boyfriend — but insult all of us. Who the hell do you think you are?"

"Listen, Sam, you don't understand . . . we were going to get back together and because of her —"

"Because of her, Eric is going to be happy and loved." (I blushed at this.) "Because of *you* he's going to be in trouble with his mother. For someone who claims that this guy is her boyfriend, you sure don't treat him like it."

"Yeah, Jenny," Allie says, coming up to stand next to Samantha. "That wasn't cool."

Jenny looks from Allie to Samantha to me and back again. "I — I —"

"I think it's time you left," Samantha says, putting her hands firmly on Jenny's shoulder and spinning her toward the door. "I think you've done enough talking for today."

Samantha pushes her toward the door — and when she is halfway through the doorway, I hear her whisper to Samantha, "But I think I might love him."

And Samantha whispers, "That's too bad. Learn how to love the next guy a little better." And gives her a final shove and shuts the door behind her.

Wow.

"Wow," Allie says, staring at Samantha like she just grew another head. Or some balls. Whatever.

"Wow is right," I say, walking toward Samantha and giving her a great big hug. "Thank you. I mean . . . well, you know . . . I just want . . ."

"Yeah," she says. "I like you too." And then she ruffles my hair like I'm six. And all I can do is nod and smile at her. I don't know who this girl is, but this is not my Samantha. I like this girl, though, and if she wants to stick around in Samantha's place for a little while, I'm OK with that.

We're all standing there smiling when it occurs to me. "What did you guys do with the food?" I'm just hoping they didn't ingest it all really quickly, like drug traffickers in a raid.

"We threw it out the window."

"What?"

"Well," Samantha says, walking toward the window, "we threw the box out the window."

We three all look out the window at the grass below. There is a smattering of food all over the lawn. Samantha hands me the phone. "You have to be there in twenty-five minutes."

"Yeah."

"At least you're packed," Allie says.

"Jesus, Allie."

"What?"

Samantha pulls Allie by the sleeve toward the door. "Let's give her a minute." I can hear them arguing outside the door, walking down the hall, and I smile.

I sit thinking about what Jenny said. She might be an idiot, but she's right — at least about this.

I think about D and how we're friends and how I should trust him enough and trust myself enough to let us be friends. Can we do that? I don't know. I don't even know if I still love him or if I just fell for Eric because D isn't around.

But I want to figure things out with Eric. That's the one

thing I'm sure of. I'm not even sure I want to leave New Horizons now. Not that I suddenly started loving vomit-food or that I like wearing four sports bras so I can skip like a clown, but I think I'd miss Allie. And Sam. And . . . Eric.

I don't know what I want anymore. It was really clear a week ago. What happened? Stupid fat camp.

I take a deep breath and pull out my cell and bring up my contacts list. I start a text message.

Am @ Fat Camp in upstate NY. Will be home tonight.

And I hit SEND, sending the text to everyone on my contact list. Including Marley. Including D. Including everyone.

EAT-IN

There are only twelve of us, mostly girls I've never talked to. We're sitting on the front steps of the cafeteria, surrounded by fat-filled products. I'm double-fisting Snickers bars (and I haven't taken a bite yet, but I'm dying to). Allie is standing in the middle of us, crooning a song — in a British accent, no less — to carbohydrates. She's actually got a really great voice and if it wasn't for her love of Brit punk and carbs, I bet she'd have some great songwriting ability too.

One of the janitorial staff is the first (and only) person to walk by during our eat-in — but he has such a terrified look on his face and takes off at a sprint toward the administration building that I think one person is all we needed.

We see Mrs. Hotra marching out of the admin building just minutes later.

"That's it?" Allie says.

"That's it," Sam responds.

"I thought it would all be so much more dramatic," Allie says, throwing a Twinkie on the floor.

"Ms. Lawrence, please pick that up and put it in the trash. We try not to litter here."

Allie blushes at being the first to be called out by Mrs. Hotra. We took care to do this right. No food packages were actually opened (or devoured) in the making of this eat-in. Could we get in trouble for having them? Probably, but that is my job. I am ready to confess — I would take the fall — I would —

"Ms. Swain, please join me in my office. Now."

The other girls look at one another and then look at me. I step off the steps and follow Mrs. Hotra down the sidewalk to the administration building.

"You just couldn't wait another twelve minutes to see me, Ms. Swain?" she said over her shoulder, walking ahead of me. If I didn't know better, I'd think she was smiling.

"I like to be productive."

"That I can tell," she says, reaching to pull open the door in front of me and holding it open so I can pass. When we reach her office, she tells me to sit in the sitting area until she's ready for me. A few minutes later Eric shows up, looking nonplussed, and sits down next to me.

UNCOMFORTABLE SILENCES AND MORE UNCOMFORTABLE CONVERSATIONS

I am feeling jittery, like I'm headed to my execution, and so my leg is bouncing up and down and accidentally brushes again Eric's leg.

"Sorry," I say, pulling my leg farther to the other side so there is absolutely no way that they could possibly touch.

"No problem," he says, pulling his legs in his direction.

"Look —" we both say at the same time.

And then we both stop and look expectantly at each other.

"I'm —" we both say, again at the same time.

I take this as a good sign. Obviously we're both about to apologize, and we'll be OK. I'm not sure how this will work, as I'm about to go home and be grounded for life. But perhaps he'll wait for me. You know, until I'm eighty and allowed out of the house again.

"You go ahead," he says.

"No, no . . . you go ahead." I smile.

"OK. I'm still mad at you."

"What?" I wasn't expecting that. I was expecting apologies and I get . . . well, not apologies.

"I'm still mad at you. I feel like you used me. You weren't honest with me. I don't even know if you were ever going to tell me that you were leaving." I must've blushed, because he nods. "I thought so. I don't know what exactly all this was for you, but it meant something to me."

I am about to respond when Eric's mom opens the door and tells us both to come in. The secretary raises her eyebrows as we walk by her desk, but she gives me a little wink and I feel — if not reassured, then at least like my life isn't quite over. Not yet. That would come when she calls my dad.

"The two of you have been causing a lot of problems lately," Mrs. Hotra says as soon as we are seated. "In fact, I'd go so far as to say that you were both having a poor influence on the other youths here."

Youths?

"So much so that I think a break might be in order. Ms. Swain, as Eric lives here, unfortunately I'm asking you to leave," she says, her hand up. "I think that this is getting out of hand and until we all have a better grip on how to . . . maneuver through these troubled waters, I think this is best. Your parents will receive a reimbursement of your tuition for the remainder of the two weeks. . . . Yes, Ms. Swain?"

"I . . . I don't know if I want to go home," I say, my lip quivering. And it surprises me to realize it's true and I'm not just saying the thing to get myself out of trouble. Although that's true too.

"I'm not sure if that is the concern at this point. At *this* point, I think it's best that you do — however — go home. I have to think about all concerned, every student here."

"Mom," Eric starts, but then stops again. He doesn't know what to say. Neither do I. We're both in the same position.

"Eric, I've made up my mind. After I call Ms. Swain's parents, you may bring her back to the train. The next train is running in an hour."

I nod. He nods. I think we're both thinking about the last conversation we might ever have together.

"Mrs. Hotra," the intercom buzzes. The secretary is buzzing through.

"Yes, Abigail?"

"Ms. Swain's stepmother is on the phone."

"Future stepmother," I quip before I realize what that means. "Wait, why *her*? Can't you talk to my father?"

"She called us, Ms. Swain," she says before pressing down the intercom button once more. "Can you put her through, please, Abigail?"

The phone clicks over a second later, and Elizabitch is on the line. "Mrs. Hotra?"

"Yes, this is Mrs. Hotra."

"Hello, I apologize for calling so late in the evening. I'm sure you're preparing for some evening festivities."

"Uh, actually . . ."

"I wouldn't call if it wasn't for a family emergency."

"A family emergency?" Mrs. Hotra says.

"Yes, Mr. Swain's sister is in the hospital. She slipped in her Choos and broke her hip."

"She slipped in her shoes?" Mrs. Hotra says, frowning.

"Choos."

"Shoes?"

"Jimmy Choos."

xl hasn't said anything about my illicit affair, my demerits, or the false alarm on the food stash. Instead I'm going home. Like I wanted. No fuss, no muss. If I had thought it could be this easy . . . I would've broken my aunt's hip days ago.

Of course, it might've helped if I actually had an aunt.

I couldn't figure out if it was Allie or Samantha on the other line, but whoever it was did a great convincing Bostonian accent. Even I was almost convinced that it was Elizabeth Butler on the phone.

"Ms. Swain — I assume that you are fully assessed of the situation."

What is the appropriate response to an aunt with a broken hip? I look at Eric and he's watching me carefully. I think he knows something is up. I gasp, "This is horrible." I cry — perhaps a moment late —"She's a dancer! Her career is going to be over!"

"Your aunt is still dancing?"

I do a quick math problem in my head. "Well, she's teaching . . . and she's a very popular teacher at the NYC ballet academy. I don't know how she'll ever recover. Ballet is her life."

I feel a stab of guilt, lying to Eric's mom about a fake aunt's ruined career as a prominent and beloved teacher.

"Eric, if Ms. Swain is ready to go, why don't you take her back to the train station?"

"Yes, ma'am."

Mrs. Hotra stands nodding behind her desk, kind of like a bobblehead, while we leave her office and walk toward the front drive where, supposedly, Eric had left the minivan, where he would take me home.

"I didn't realize you had a ballerina in the family," he says, shooting me a sideways glance as we walk side by side.

"I didn't realize it either."

"A ballerina?" Samantha says in a very snooty Bostonian accent.

"That was you?" I ask, floored. It really is a very good accent.

"I fancy myself something of an actress," she says, pulling me into a hug.

"That's great," Eric says, taking my suitcases from me and throwing it in the backseat. Wow, great. Someone is overly emotional.

"He'll get over it. He's happy. He really is," Samantha says, giving me another squeeze before letting me go. I nod happily. I know she's right. He'll forgive me. If I get the chance to apologize.

THE LONGEST DRIVE EVER

Look, I'm sorry," I blurt out, five minutes into our drive to the station.

"Yeah," he huffs. "You sound sorry."

I look out the window, rolling it down all the way so I can stick my head out. I love nature. Sort of. Not the smelly kind. It's night and it's really dark out; there is a weird buzzing sound in the distance, I think they might be bugs. I stick my head back inside and roll up the window.

"I mean it," I say, pulling my head back to face him. "I'm sorry. I didn't mean to get you involved in all of this."

"Did you ever think I wanted to get involved?"

"Huh?"

He pulls the minivan over sharply to the side of the road and throws it into park.

"Holy shit!" I scream. Minivans are not three-wheelers. I swear I was five seconds away from death from Mr. Emo tipping the van.

"Look, did you ever think that I might want to be involved?

200

I might want to know what's up with you. I might actually *want* to know what your plans are . . . and God forbid that I want to say good-bye before you jet back to NYC to be with that guy that you think is so much better for you than I am."

"Eric —"

"No, answer me this," he says, not turning to face me. He's still facing the road and his knuckles are white — he's holding the steering wheel so tightly. "Do you love him?"

"Him who?" I ask.

He gives me a look.

"No."

"No?" he says. "HA!"

"HA?!" I say back. "You asked me a question and I responded."

"I wanted an honest response."

"And I gave you one."

Now I'm looking out the window and calculating how long it would take me to walk to the station from where we are: One girl, going .5 miles per hour, on a long, dark wooded road. Add some suitcases, one Gucci bag, and three potential murderers . . . how long does it take before they find the body? Word problem, anyone?

"Look, I don't think I love him," I say. "I mean, I love him as a friend. I think. I just want the opportunity to talk to him face-to-face. I wanted to go and see him to be sure."

This honesty racket is so totally overrated.

"It means a lot to you?" he asks.

"Yeah."

"Fine, I'll drive you," he says, turning the ignition — the van sparking to life once more. He turns the lights on and pulls back onto the road.

"What?"

"I'm driving you home."

"You're crazy," I say, but I'm smiling like an absolute fiend. He still loves me. He's still perfect. Well . . . perfect for me.

"I must be," he mutters, pulling the van up to speed.

Manhattan is a 4.2-hour drive. I call up the MapQuest directions on my phone; it's going to be a long drive. It takes Eric four turns to get onto the highway because he refuses to ask for directions. We have our second fight before he finally pulls into a gas station and makes me get out and find out where the highway is.

He calls his mother and leaves a message saying he isn't going to be home. I ask him if he is going to get into trouble and he shrugs. "Sometimes you ask for forgiveness because you know you'll never get permission . . . and if it's worth it . . ."

I smile. I like that I am worth it.

The first hour we spend in the minivan we argue over what to play. I want to use my iPod to play Chicago or some other girly pop. HE wants to play hard rock. I can't sing along to hard rock. We turn the radio off.

Then we talk about everything but why we're driving to NYC. We talk about school and our ambitions and goals. We talk about our favorite movies (Me: *Love Me If You Dare* — a French film about screwed-up relationships. Him: *Teenage Mutant Ninja Turtles*. I'm not even kidding). We realize that we both love Bruce Willis. He admits that he might be a little weird about how much. . . . We discover that we both lost our front teeth at the same time and lisped for almost six months before they began to grow back in. I tell him more about my mother dying. He tells me more about his father leaving. I tell him about how much I like to play volleyball in gym class, even though it's seriously uncool. He tells me how much he enjoyed his art class even though he was expected to take all these AP classes and never get below a B, how much he wanted to take more electives.

A little while later we find an old eighties station on the radio and are both singing along. Badly. Apparently neither of us can sing. We bond over bad vocals.

Three hours in, we are friends again. And I love him.

By the time we are about half an hour outside the city, I am ready to kill him again.

"Tell me about this guy," he says.

"I'd rather not."

"I'd rather you did."

"Why?" I ask.

"Because I'm extremely jealous and want to gauge the possibility that you'll see him, fall madly back in love with him, and I'll lose you to some douche-bag New Yorker who wears a bloody kimono."

Whoa, never heard him swear before. "He's British."

"Jesus Christ."

"What?"

"Of course he's British. Why wouldn't he be?"

I just smile and don't say anything.

Twenty minutes of silence later he babbles something like, "I bet he's tall too."

Another fifteen minutes later, as we enter the city, he says, "He better not call you darling, sweetheart, or any of those other stupid pet names British men think are cute."

I turn toward the window so he can't see my face.

I call D from the car and wake him up. I don't even care at this point and he finally wakes up when he realizes I'm in the area. "What are you doing here?"

"Oh, I don't know — I live here maybe."

"I know but I was coming to pick you up today."

"I texted you."

He is quiet for a moment before responding, "I got it."

"I'm sorry I lied to you."

"Come over," he says. He asks me to give him five minutes and then I should come up. I tell him it would take us that long to park anyway.

"Us? Park?"

I tell him I'd explain when I saw him and hung up the phone.

"So I get to actually meet this guy?" Eric says, looking for a parking spot.

"Yeah, looks like."

"Swell."

"Be nice."

"I'm always nice," he says. Which is mostly true, but I guess if he was going to be not nice, this was the time he would do so.

We walk up to D's building. The doorman greets me and I hear (if not see) Eric roll his eyes. "Of course there is a doorman."

Wait till he sees my place. I am worried.

We take the elevator up.

"Of course it's the penthouse."

And the door opens right into the apartment. I try to see it how Eric must be seeing it. "Listen," he says, pulling me around to face him. "I just want you to remember one thing."

"What?"

He pulls me closer and kisses me, and I feel everything he wants me to remember. I think I'm curling and twisting on the inside.

"Ahem." I can hear D clear his throat.

Eric pulls away slightly but doesn't let go of me. "Remember he didn't know what he had. You're perfect. You're amazing and everything a guy could ask for. I knew it before I even met you."

I look at him and wonder.

"Ahem!" D clears his throat a little louder.

I pull myself out of Eric's grasp, but not before I see the slightly smug look on his face. This doesn't look like it's going to go well.

I don't quite understand the look on D's face when I turn around to face him. Later, I'd realize that it was a mixture of possessiveness, envy, and perhaps curiosity. None of which was jealousy, which is what I used to hope for, but it was more than he had ever shown me before.

I'm looking at him and thinking, *Did I really love him?* And then he walks over and gives me a wraparound hug that is very D in an overwhelming D way. I'm about to fall over when he gives me a loud smack on the cheek and says, "How are you, darling?"

I hear a snort from behind me, and while I'm still in the precarious position of having to hold on to D for my life, lest I fall, ass-first, onto a very hard-looking marble foyer, D looks over me at Eric. Looks him up and down in a way that I've only seen British people and women in *Vogue* do, and asks, "Who's your little friend?"

I struggle my way out of his arms and right myself. My bags are already on the floor, but I'll worry about that later. "D, this is Eric. Eric, this is my best friend, D."

I watch D's face as I introduce them.

"Nice apartment," Eric says.

"Nice shoes," D says, pointedly looking at Eric's brightly colored Adidas originals.

"Nice outfit. From Riley's description, I was expecting a kimono."

"Hmm. I suppose I should be flattered I received a description at all," he says, turning his back on us and walking farther into the apartment. "I didn't even know you existed."

I gasp a little, but Eric just has a wry grin on his face, and we both follow D into the sitting room — where we sit side by side on the couch. I feel like this is worse than sitting in front of Mrs. Hotra once she knew that I had basically mouth-assaulted her son in my tent at New Horizons. This is probably worse than it will be when I introduce Eric to my father. *If* I introduce Eric to my father. I meant to say *if.*

D sits on a chair, his legs crossed, ankle at his knee, and looks at us both. "So, what have you kids been up to?" I feel more than see Eric's smirk, and in an attempt to head off any future collisions, I jump up and ask D if I could talk to him in the other room.

207

There are a lot of bug-eye movements and head jerks to the right. He finally agrees and follows me away from Eric, who looks small and out of place in the Hammond family sitting room.

We stand in the kitchen, the silence positively deafening.

Why is it that I could be fabulous in all things . . . but not here, not now? Not with this guy who has been my best friend for years?

"Do you like this guy?" he says when we're out of hearing range.

"Yeah."

"He's not your type."

"I know," I say, smiling. He looks at me, surprised.

"Wow, you really like him," he says, then runs his hand through his hair. I don't feel a thing, which bothers me. "What about us?"

"Oh, we can still make out," I say.

"Don't do that, Riley," he says.

"Don't do what?"

"Don't make this into something you know it isn't. Are we OK? You're my best friend. I still need you to be my best friend."

I look at him. No coyness, just a blank stare, and I feel like I want to vomit. "I still want that," I say softly. "But I lied to you."

"Yes, and the public flogging shall commence at high noon,"

he says, and then his voice drops. "I just don't want this thing hanging over us."

"Meaning?"

"The thing where we kissed. I don't want to constantly be wondering whenever we talk or whenever we hang out if this is a thing."

"Don't worry about it," I say. "I don't think I was being honest with myself when it came to you. I thought I loved you, but I think I was wrong."

"How do you know you're being honest with yourself now?" he asks.

"What?"

"I mean, you say you were in love with me," he says, and before I can correct him he finishes, "but then you say you really weren't. How do you know it's gone?"

"Gone? I'm not sure it was ever there," I say.

"Well, I think it's worth checking, for the both of us," he says.

He puts his hands on my shoulders and pulls me in close. I, on autopilot, tilt my chin up and kiss him. Then the autopilot begins speaking in my brain as D kisses me:

He's actually a very good kisser. He doesn't spit.

I wonder what it would be like if I really loved him. And then I wonder about how much has changed in such a short week, but then again, I hadn't kissed Eric the last time D and I were in this position.

There has been a lot of kissing going on lately.

Kids do like their kissing. . . .

And then I start to laugh.

D pulls away. "Not exactly the reaction I was going for."

"Oh God, I'm so sorry, D, it's just that . . . It's . . ."

"Riley, don't worry about it," he says, covering my lips with the tip of my finger. He smiles at me and then starts to laugh. Giggle, really.

"I'm sorry," I say. "But did it feel like . . ." And then I start to giggle too.

"You're a good kisser," he says. "But I didn't feel — I mean, I love you."

"And I love you."

"But . . ."

"Yeah."

"I guess I always knew you'd find a guy you really like," he says, and I'm all ears. "I mean, I thought he'd be taller and I didn't realize he'd paint his nails."

I smile. Big.

"But I'm glad you found someone. Just don't be one of those girls."

"Those girls?"

"The kind that ignores their best friends just because they fall in love."

We smile at each other, shyly, and I think it'll be fine. We're going to be friends again, perhaps even better friends. I'll be a better friend. I make that promise in my head.

We walk back into the sitting room and Eric is gone. My phone buzzes in my pocket and I pull it out.

Mr. Right texted me.

**Perhaps it's time for me to make a graceful exit.
So it's not messy.**

WHAT?

I text him back, and all I get back is You kissed him.

How do you write the guy you like that you just tongue-kissed your best friend to make sure you were really in love with the guy you like?

I try calling him, but he doesn't pick up.

"He's not picking up!"

"Tell me what happened," D says.

I want to cry about it so I tell him the entire story — perhaps highlighting the responses made a little too much.

"That's everything?" he asks.

I sniff and say yes, that's everything (mostly — I do leave out a few of the more psycho foot-stomping incidents, because even now, only twenty minutes later, I can see how psychotic foot stomping can be. What is WRONG with me?).

"Well, this is easy," he says.

"Really?"

"Yes," he continues. "You're psychotic. I mean, a guy will be led by his dick for only so long. Eventually his brain kicks in. And yes, it does happen."

"That part is obvious, but the part that confuses me . . ."

(How he could possibly not love me?)

"Is how you could possibly think you could do all that to him and have him still?"

"What do you mean?"

"He loves you. You love him. You acted psycho," he says. "I personally would've told you to screw off."

And it hits me.

I'm brought low by the truth of it all.

"You can't keep doing this, to yourself or to him," he says.

"But what am I supposed to do now?" I ask. Sniff. Cry. Moan. Bemoan. WAIL.

"Let him go. Or go get him back."

"But I don't know how."

"You'll figure it out," he says, rumpling my hair. "Stay here. I'll call a car and take you home." And my tombstone would say: "Riley Swain, the great and fabulous, brought low by a boy. A boy from upstate New York." It is too sad to contemplate.

D gets out of the car, holds the door open for me, and tells me, "Go get him, tiger," which I take to heart.

Except Marley is standing on my front steps.

"Oh, hey, D," she says, fixing her hair. Tramp. "Riley, I was just about to knock and ask your parents if you were in."

I sigh. I look at D and he just shrugs at me. No help, great best friend.

"What's up, Marley?" I ask.

D cuts in, "Ladies, as much as I'm into all sorts of fun little girl-on-girl catfights, I'm going to excuse myself." We both look at him with pissed-off expressions. "Riley, call me later. Marley." He nods and then gets back into the car — it speeds off so fast that it makes my head spin.

"Chicken," Marley says, watching the taillights, and I smile. I think it's the first thing she ever said that I full-heartedly agree with.

"How long have you been here, an hour?"

"Almost two," she says, stretching out her legs.

"Did you rat me out to the 'rents?"

"Not yet," she says, pulling a lip gloss out of her bag, applying it, and smacking her lips.

"They're not home, you know," I say.

"That's fine, I can always catch them later," she says. *And I can always send a dirty video of you to your parents . . .* I don't say this. I'm a new Riley. I'm a new Riley. I'm a new Riley.

"Look, I'm sorry I made out with Timothy."

She doesn't look up.

"I'm sorry. It was horrible of me. I just . . ." I sit down

and look at her. "You told everyone I was fat and going to fat camp."

"Well, you were."

I give her a look.

"I don't mean you were fat, but you did go to a fat camp. And you lied to us all about it."

"Of course I did."

She looks down. "You're supposed to be my best friend and you don't tell me anything."

Excuse me? What? "We're not really best friends, Marley."

She looks at me and I can't believe it, but she has tears in her eyes. Or maybe her LASIK went wrong? "I know you don't think we're friends, but you're my friend. Except you treat me like shit all the time, and I can't seem to do anything that makes you like me, and so I try to be like you. And that seems to get your attention. You like me when I'm a bitch."

My face goes slack and I don't really know what to say.

"And then you went after Timothy and I realized that you really do hate me, and it's not just an act."

"Why would you think it was an act?" I ask.

"Because you're the same way to D, and I know you adore him."

"What way?"

"You treat him like you hate him, but I know it's only because you love him so much and that you're scared that he's going to reject you so you reject yourself first," she says, sniffing.

"Someone has had too much therapy," I say.

"True," she says. "Doesn't make it any less true."

I sit and think about that. "You always act like you're better than me," I say.

She shrugs.

"You always flirt with D."

"You KISSED the boy I like!"

"Yeah," I say. "I'm sorry about that. I mean . . . I think you should still make out with him, if you want."

"I already did."

"What?" I say, screeching. Ew — I made out with Tim for no reason?

"I like him. I really like him," she says. "And I told him that if he goes within two feet of you again I would have my daddy get him blacklisted at all the Ivy League schools with crew teams."

I'm shocked by the laughter that erupts from my mouth; so is she — she smiles at me, almost shyly.

"Good for you," I say. "Are you going to rat me out?"

"No," she says.

"I think we should go to Starbucks and grab a latte. Just the two of us."

She nods.

Why do I feel like everything and everyone has changed in the six days since I left Manhattan and then returned? Perhaps because it has. Marley gets up and gives me a hug and walks away, down the street to her place, and I watch as she goes until I can't see her behind a tall guy wearing a beaver hat who is walking behind her.

I take stock of the situation. I'm a smart girl. I should be able to figure out how to find the guy I like. I'm fabulous. After finding the guy I like, I should be able to figure out how to seduce him.

How hard can it be to seduce someone you've already fooled around with?

Now that my self-confidence is boosted (too bad I don't have my iPod with me, I could be playing the *Rocky* theme song), I decide I have to talk to him. I try calling again but his cell keeps going straight to voice mail. This might take a bit of a sacrifice.

I sit on the stoop a little while longer, thinking about what I want from Eric and what I want from D and what Marley wants from me. Which still blows my mind. I don't know if I can ever be friends, real friends, with Marley — but who knows, she was my *best* enemy. Perhaps there is more room for change there?

I get up and walk into the house, opening the front door with my spare key.

"Finally decided to come in?" My dad is sitting in his chair, facing the front hall so that he could see me as I walked by. I scream, so surprised am I to see him and Elizabitch sitting there on a Saturday morning.

"Dad . . . uh . . ."

"Riley, come in and sit down."

He motions toward the seat to one side, which I climb onto, tucking my feet beneath me and curling into the over-stuffed leather chair. "What's going on?"

And I start crying again. Elizabitch looks at both of us and excuses herself from the room. As she walks by, she puts her hand on my shoulder and gives me a light squeeze.

Seriously, what is happening to NYC? Is there something in the water? At least her hair is still a frizzy mess, so I know aliens haven't come down and taken control of her body.

My dad doesn't say anything. I don't know what he could say — he's never been really good with crying women. I mean, I don't cry around him, but Elizabitch always cries and it usually gets her what she wants. I bet she cried about getting married and that's why he proposed.

So he doesn't say anything, but instead he gets up and comes around to me, pulling me out of the chair and wrapping his arms around me. I cry into his shirt and tie, which are probably going to be ruined, but I can't stop. These are not small tears. These are those sobs you get when you are little, when you can't seem to contain the amount of emotion releasing itself from your body. I am two shades away from breaking down completely, or throwing up on the Oriental rug.

He sits down in the chair, pulling me onto his lap.

"I'll crush your legs," I tell him, my hand on the arm of the chair.

"Come here, I'm not old and decrepit."

He settles me into his lap, and has his arms around me, and laughs a little when I say, "Well, you're not decrepit."

After a few minutes I relax and my crying stops. A few minutes later I am breathing normally again. A few minutes after that, I get up and sit on the floor, where I feel more comfortable.

"Want to tell me what happened, pet?" he asks, his hand on my head.

"I met a boy."

"A boy?"

"Yeah, at New Horizons. He is the headmistress's son."

"And?" I can feel his hand tense, but I don't look up. It's embarrassing enough to have this conversation with my own father, let alone look him in the eye while doing it. But I have to do it, I have to get back to Eric and make this right.

"His name is Eric. He's shorter than I am. And blond. And paints his nails."

"Black?"

"Blond."

"No, what color does he paint his nails?"

"Red."

"Hmm. OK, go ahead." He motions for me to continue.

"He's not at all my type, but he told me that maybe my type was wrong for me," I say.

"I like him."

"Dad, I didn't finish the story," I cry.

"Sorry, go ahead."

And I do. I tell him the whole story, a little more honestly than I told D. I mean, D's my best friend. But this is my dad. I tell him how I was scared that I love him and why. I tell him about how I don't want to lose him and how I want to go back. I tell him that my cc was canceled.

"Oh, that I know."

"You do?"

"Yes, I closed it."

"WHY?" I howled.

"Perhaps because of a three-thousand-dollar charge for Dahlia's Day Spa?"

I have the decency to blush like a bright red tomato.

"So, now you think you didn't hate it there?"

"I mean, I hated it there. Or at least I think I did. But I love him. And I love everyone else there. And I'm not sure if I can learn anything or if I want to change. I mean, I don't think I need to change. I like how I look."

I stop automatically. It's just not OK for a girl who is overweight to like how she looks. I mean, I can tell myself that I do, and I can tell my friends that I do, but I don't know what my dad will say. He's the one who sent me, after all.

"I didn't think that you needed to go either. Elizabeth thought it would be good for you."

"Figures," I say. So I was right, she was trying to get me out of the way.

"She had gone when she was your age. She says she made her best friends there and it helped her to be OK with who she was. No matter what. When I told her I was worried about you, she suggested that it might be a good solution," he admits. "I didn't really know what else to do."

"You were worried about me?" I ask, looking up at him. "Why didn't you say anything?"

"I didn't know what to say, which sounds like a load of bull poop right now." I roll my eyes at the lack of profanity, but he ignores me and keeps going. "But sometimes you're not the easiest person to talk to."

"I could say the same thing for you, Mr. CrackBerry."

He nods. "Let's both make an effort to fix this."

"Fix what?"

"Our relationship. I mean, there are a lot of things that you should come to me to discuss. And the things you can't, well, you can always go to Elizabeth."

"Um, pass."

"Riley," he says. "I do love her. I want her to be part of our family — but . . . But if it's not something you can see through, then it's not going to happen. I'm not sure if that's right or not but, well, we've already pushed off the date for over a year because I wasn't sure if you were ready for a stepmother."

"You pushed off the date? I'm sure Elizabeth loved that."

"It was Elizabeth's idea."

Damn and damn.

"I don't know. I mean, I'm OK with you marrying her. I don't care. But I don't know if I can like her," I say, and he looks thoughtful. "But if she's open to it, I'm willing to try again. On Switzerland."

"Switzerland?"

"Neutral ground."

"I see," he says. "That's fair."

"And what about . . ."

"Well, if you want to go back and you think it's for more than just . . . I'll go with you to the station." I jump up and hug him tightly as he laughs. This is what having a dad feels like.

"Don't think you're not grounded, because you are. The minute you get home, you're really, really grounded."

Damn.

"I thought we were finally bonding," I say, smiling sweetly. "Let's not ruin it with talk of punishment or grounding."

"And you're going to work off the money you spent and wasted in chores or a part-time job after school."

Double damn.

*　　*　　*

I am so excited on my way back to upstate NY (seriously, I can't believe I said that. Seriously, I can't believe I meant it) that I am jittery in my seat. The guy sitting in the seat next to me, holding a newspaper, gives me a really dirty look when I jostle his shoulder. I smile as sweetly as I can, but he still huffs. Grump.

When I am thirty minutes away from the station I call the only person who I know has a car and who I thought would actually pick me up.

Ms. Wilhelm is waiting for me on the platform when the train pulls in. She smiles and waves as I walk up. I still feel a little awkward, but she talks right over any potential awkward silences and pulls me in for a one-armed hug at her side as we walk to her car.

"A Toyota Corolla."

"Yup," she said, unlocking the doors as I step in. I miss the minivan. "Eric got back a few hours ago."

"Oh?" I say, trying to appear nonchalant.

"Yup."

"And . . ."

"And what, Riley?"

I huff, "Is he OK? Did you see him? Did his mother kill him?"

"Yes. Yes. No."

"You're doing this on purpose," I say, giving her a slightly dirty look.

"Yup," she says, starting to laugh. "Tell me about Eric."

"You know Eric," I say.

"Tell me about the Eric you know."

We drive the rest of the way to the New Horizons campus. I talk about the Eric I know and how he isn't my type, but how I don't even know if I have a type anymore. And how he is so different and how he makes me feel so comfortable with who I am.

"You know what it's like?" I begin. "It's like great friends make you see who you really are and great love makes you see who you want to be. D saw me for whatever I am, and accepted that. I think that Eric sees the same stuff that D sees, but he loves me for it and thinks it's wonderful and that I'm wonderful. And so I want to be wonderful for him. I just feel like I've known him forever."

"I think that's a lot to think about," she says. I make a face, because she sounds like a therapist, and she shrugs. Old habits are hard to break, I suppose.

"He's mad at me," I say. "I think he thinks I don't like him."

"I think that'll be an easy thing to fix, as long as you're honest."

"Yeah," I say as we pull onto the drive and up in front of the administration building.

"Well, after you talk to Mrs. Hotra, you'll be able to get settled back in. I know you have at least two friends who are excited that you've returned."

"Does Mrs. Hotra know?"

"Know what?" She gives me a blank look.

"That my aunt didn't . . . I mean, that I don't . . ." I want to be honest, but I'm not sure how much honesty is a good idea here. Does therapy have the same confidentiality as lawyer-client privilege? Does it count if it's in a Toyota?

"I don't know what you're talking about," she says, and then winks, and I start. Oh, OK. I smile and thank her for the ride. She says she'll see me around and pulls away in her car, probably headed home . . . to what, I wonder. To where? There is so much I don't know about her, or about a lot of people. She's got this entire life that I know nothing about; she might even have a boyfriend. She might be in love with someone. Crazy.

I walk into the administration office and Abigail smiles at me and tells me to "go right in."

"You've decided to return to us," Mrs. Hotra says.

"Mrs. Hotra, I just want to say . . . I know. I mean, I kind of feel like I've lied to everyone and it's gotten me nowhere. But I don't know if I can change just like that, but I do want to try. I want to stay. And I love your son." I scrunch up my eyes so that if her head pops off or explodes, I won't be witness to it.

"Unfortunately, Ms. Swain, I feel that the original issue that we discussed is still a concern."

I look up and she's marking something in her calendar and not paying attention to me at all.

"Mrs. Hotra? Is there any way I can change your mind?" I ask.

"Unfortunately, I've already discussed this with your father, earlier today."

"You did?" I ask. "But I talked to him and he didn't mention anything to me."

"He thought it might be helpful for you to return and fix your own problems."

"What?" I ask.

"Well, unfortunately, the rules here at New Horizons necessitate that we ask you to leave for the remainder of this session."

I nod.

"But I think you're a nice girl, Riley. I think you'll be fine."

I blush at that.

"Please feel free to spend the rest of the day on campus saying your good-byes."

Um. OK. I start to leave and have my hand on the doorknob when she calls me back. "I think he likes you a lot, Riley." I blush. This is his mom — I mean, you would blush too. "I think you need to talk to him and make him listen."

"I will, Mrs. Hotra. I will."

I head back to the dorms, without my bags. I knock on the door to my room and Sam opens it, then screams.

"Oh my God! You're back." She rushes over and grabs me into a hug. "How was it? What happened? What's going on?"

"Eric is mad at me. D and I are friends. I had a good talk with my dad. Ms. Wilhelm isn't crazy and Mrs. Hotra definitely is crazy."

"Sweet, you're back?"

"No, I'm still suspended, but I was told that I could say my good-byes, if I wanted to. . . ." I let my voice drag out.

"I'm glad you're back — even for a little while. I didn't have a chance to write down all your information, and when I'm home over Christmas we can see each other."

"What? Where's home?"

"My parents live in the city," Samantha says, pulling out some paper.

"You're from the city?" I say, gawking.

"Yeah," she says. Well. That's a shocker.

We walk arm in arm to the dining hall. My eyes float around looking for Eric, but I only spy Jenny, who mutters, "You're back?"

"You're observant." And we keep walking and sit down

with Allie, who is in the middle of a crazy story about David Bowie; her hands are waving and she jumps up and plays some air guitar while the rest of us just shake our heads at her.

Everything seems great. I'm among friends again.

But . . . something is missing.

"Riley, Eric," Samantha says, pointing over my right shoulder and out the front window. He's sitting down in the back of the buildings underneath the trees that we had been sitting under before.

"I'll be right back, guys," I say, and then walk out the building to meet him, but he's no longer there. But I have an idea where he might have gone.

I approach the dock and see his back silhouetted against the lake and sky. I walk up quietly, scared that if he really hears me coming, he might jump up at the last minute and make a mad dash for it.

He doesn't move, even when I stand next to him for several minutes, so I sit down on the planks next to his, happy for my Diesel jeans — that I can be comfortable. It's chilly out and I'm snuggled up in a Columbia sweatshirt, despite the flip-flops I'm hoping won't fly off my feet into the murky water. But Eric is sitting there, his legs crossed under him Indian-style, looking out at the water.

I am preparing what I want to say, filing the right thoughts and the right words into the right order, prevaricating, really.

"Why'd you come back?" he asks softly.

"I wanted to lose those last twenty pesky pounds."

He looks at me. OK, not the moment for joking.

"I had unfinished business," I say.

"So you're back?"

"Actually, no. Your mom kicked me out."

"Seriously?"

"Yeah, but she also said you like me."

"Mothers are known to say crazy things."

"Yeah."

He's still looking at me. Boring his eyes into me. "That's all?"

"No, I missed Samantha and I think she needs me. Her wardrobe, at least, really needs me."

"Is that all?"

"No, I really wanted to try cottage cheese."

"Riley . . ."

"I think I love you."

"What?" he says, his eyebrows springing up and then burrowing together again.

"I think I love you, although I'm not really sure. See, I thought I was in love with D — but it turns out that I just thought I was and it wasn't real. But I didn't know for sure until

I kissed him. And realized that I didn't love him. But then I didn't know what to do, but he's just my best friend."

"You needed to stick your tongue in his mouth again to know that?"

Ouch.

"Look," he says, "I'm glad you've had an epiphany when it comes to whether or not you love D, but I'm not sure what that has to do with me."

"It means that I didn't realize I didn't love him, couldn't love him, until I realized that I might love someone else. You," I say. "I mean you. I mean, I think I could love you. It's just that we've only known each other for such a short time, and I feel like I've lied to you this entire time."

"Um," he says.

"I know that's a weird thing to say, but I'm a little scared that I don't know the difference."

"Actually," he says, looking out over the water, "I have a small confession to make."

"Huh? What?"

"We've known each other for a few months now."

"Oh yeah?" I laugh, but he's not laughing. He's serious. "What do you mean we've known each other?"

"Well, we didn't know each other, we had never met . . . but we've been talking."

"I'm not following."

"I'm Thebigun17."

"That's how you pronounce that?" I blurt. "Wait . . . you're . . ."

"Yeah," he says, and he has the grace to look sheepish.

"You've been lying to me this whole time?"

"Sort of, I mean, I tried to tell you," he says.

"How? When? How hard is it to say, 'Hi, Riley, I'm Thebigun17?' And what kind of screen name is that?"

"Riley, I tried . . . I mean, I told you I MySpaced you, and that's how I got your screen name . . . and . . ."

"Oh my God, and that's how I met Thebigun17. I didn't even think of it."

He shrugs.

"I thought I loved you and I didn't even know I had been talking to you."

"Yeah, sorry about that."

He sits staring at the water for a moment, and I wonder and think about the conversations we've had. All the stories I've told him and all the advice he's given me.

"You *think* you might love me? Is there a way you could possibly know?"

I smile, take a deep — shaky — breath and say, "I'm not sure, that was before this whole stalker confession."

"I figured, but if I hadn't confessed . . . What were you thinking . . ."

"I thought maybe you'd let me kiss you. Not forgive me or

anything, because I was a total prat. But, like, as an experiment. To see . . ."

He turns and, putting his arm around me, pulls me down to the dock in his arms.

"Do you use this line on all the guys?" he asks, looking at me — brushing his fingertips over my face. I feel warm and safe and real.

"Only the kissing one. Not the love one. And only if they stalked me."

"Are you sure?" he says, propping himself over me. Looking into my eyes. And I see love there.

"I'm sure," I say, pulling his head down until his mouth meets mine.

And my mind goes blank.

EPILOGUE

THEBIGUN17: How was your day?

RILEDUP: Who cares? You're going to be here in two days!!!

THEBIGUN17: Yeah, yeah.

RILEDUP: You're not excited?!

THEBIGUN17: Oh, I'm hopping in my seat. You just can't tell because you can't see me.

RILEDUP: Liar.

THEBIGUN17: Would you call me a liar if I said I can't wait to kiss you again?

RILEDUP: No, but that's a given.

THEBIGUN17: Why's that?

RILEDUP: Because I'm so fabulous, how could you resist?

THEBIGUN17: lol. True enough.

RILEDUP: <3 You.

I have an important theory about love. My theory is that if you fall in love with the right guy, and this guy is everything you're looking for (and the list is short and simple: does he love me? does he make me feel fabulous?) . . . and if you fall in love with him . . . you both should have the decency to live happily ever after.

Riley Swain
xoxo

ACKNOWLEDGMENTS

Writing this book was not a solitary endeavor. Publishing it took a small army (and three semi-nude male models, but those were just for show). I'd like to thank the following people for their invaluable help and guidance . . .

. . . to literary agent Stephen Barbara, for telling me it went to seed after page 23, for being an amazing friend, a patient author's advocate, and for always being willing to listen to me whine about boys, work, or life in general. I adore you and owe you dinner.

. . . to my editor Aimee Friedman, for loving it first and then using her mad editing skills to make it a book worthy of her affections. Every great change (and the fact that it's all in one tense) starts and ends with her attention and mighty skill; any flaws are my own.

. . . to Abby McAden and the FABULOUS team at Scholastic, thank you for making this dream come true.

. . . to my friend and fellow author Ted Malawer, for going above and beyond, whenever it mattered, for helping me keep things in perspective while making me laugh harder and longer than is advisable or particularly healthy.

. . . to my friend Michael Stearns, for "less talking, more writing" appointments at the Tea Lounge. I owe the (on deadline) completion of this book to you. A man of more and varied talents, I never have met—it's an honor and a privilege.

. . . to my family, who would kill me if I didn't add them here. Although they didn't really do anything except ask if I would be on Oprah. But a special shout-out to my Mom, I love you.

And, finally, to my boys, who became the basis for every good story I've ever told. Thanks for giving me something to whine about.